A bitter divorce is only the beginning. First the father hires thugs to kidnap his son. Then the mother hires Spenser to get the boy back.

But as soon as Spenser senses the lay of the land, he decides to do some kidnapping of his own. With a contract out on his life, he heads for the Maine woods, determined to give a puny fifteen-year-old a crash course in survival and to beat his dangerous opponents at their own brutal game.

ROBERT B. PARKER

EARLY AUTUMN

A BOOK-OF-THE-MONTH CLUB
ALTERNATE SELECTION

Books by Robert B. Parker Available from Dell

EARLY AUTUMN

Robert B. Parker

A DELL BOOK

Published by
Dell Publishing
a division of
Bantam Doubleday Dell Publishing Group, Inc.
666 Fifth Avenue
New York, New York 10103

For David Parker and Daniel Parker,
with the respect and admiration of their father,
who grew up with them.

ISBN: 0-440-12214-7

Reprinted by arrangement with Delacorte Press/Seymour Lawrence

Printed in the United States of America

Two Previous Editions

October 1987

25 24 23 22 21 20 19 18 17 16 15

RAD

CHAPTER 1

The urban renewers had struck again. They'd evicted me, a fortune-teller, and a bookie from the corner of Mass. Ave. and Boylston, moved in with sandblasters and bleached oak and plant hangers, and last I looked appeared to be turning the place into a Marin County whorehouse. I moved down Boylston Street to the corner of Berkeley, second floor. I was half a block from Brooks Brothers and right over a bank. I felt at home. In the bank they did the same kind of stuff the fortune-teller and the bookie had done. But they dressed better.

I was standing in the window of my office looking out at a soft rainy January day with the temperature in the high fifties and no sign of snow. To the right across Boylston I could see Bonwit Teller. To the left Police Headquarters. In Bonwit's windows there were mannequins wearing tight leather clothes and chains. Police headquarters leaned more to Dacron. In the window bay of the advertising agency across the street a young black-haired woman in high-waisted gray trousers leaned over a drawing board. Her back was toward the window.

"My compliments to your tailor," I said out loud. My voice sounded odd in the empty room. The black-haired woman went away and I sat at my desk and looked at the picture of Susan Silverman. It was the blowup of a color picture taken last summer in her backyard. Her tanned face and pink blouse were bright against the dark green of the muted trees. I was still looking at Susan's face when my office door opened and a client came in carrying a belted poplin raincoat over one arm.

She said, "Mr. Spenser?"

I said, "I knew my clientele would upgrade when I moved in over a bank."

She smiled wonderfully at me. She had blond hair that contrasted handsomely with her black eyes and dark eyebrows. She was small and very trim and elegant. She had on a tailored black suit and vest, white shirt, black bow tie with long ends like Brett Maverick used to wear, and black boots with very high narrow heels. She was wearing gold and it looked real: gold earrings, gold watch, gold chains around the neck, gold chain bracelets, a wide gold wedding band, and a large diamond in a gold setting. I was optimistic about my fee.

She said, "You are Mr. Spenser?"

I said, "Yes," and stood up and held a chair for her. She had a precise walk and a very nicely integrated figure and she sat erect in the chair. I went around behind my desk again and sat down and smiled. Time was they started to undress when I smiled, but I guess the smile had lost a step. The black eyes looked at me very carefully. The hands folded still in the lap. Ankles crossed, face serious. She looked at my face, both shoulders, my chest, and as much of my stomach as showed behind the desk.

I said, "I have a puckered scar on the back of my right, ah, thigh where a man shot me about three years ago."

She nodded.

"My eyes look maybe a little funny because I used to be a fighter. That's scar tissue."

"Apparently people hit you in the nose quite often too," she said.

"Yes," I said.

She looked at me some more. At my arms, at my hands. Would I seem forward if I offered to drop trou? Probably.

I said, "Got all my teeth though. See." I bared them.

"Mr. Spenser," she said. "Tell me why I should employ you."

"Because if you don't you'll have wasted all this sizing up," I said. "You'll have spent all this time impressing me with your no-nonsense elegance and your perfect control and gone away empty."

She studied my forehead.

"And I look very dashing in a deer stalker and a trench coat."

She looked directly at me and shook her head slightly.

"And I have a gun," I said. I took it off my hip and showed it to her.

She turned her head away and looked out my window, where it had gotten dark and shiny with the lights glistening off the rain.

I put the gun away and clasped my hands and rested my elbows on the arms of my chair and propped my chin. I let the chair tip back on its spring and I sat and waited.

"Mr. Spenser, do you have time to waste like this," she said.

"Yes, I do," I said.

"Well, I do not," she said and I lip-synched the words with her as she said them. That annoyed her.

"Don't you want the job?" she said.

"I don't know," I said. "I don't know what the job is."

"Well, I want some evidence of your qualifications before I discuss it with you."

"Hell, lady, I showed you my scar tissue and my gun. What else do you need?"

"This is a sensitive job. It is not a matter of guns. It involves a child."

"Maybe you should get hold of Dr. Spock."

Silence. She looked at my hands where my chin was resting.

"Your hands are very strong-looking," she said.

"Want to see me crack a walnut?" I said.

"Are you married?" she said.

"No."

She smiled again. It was a good one. Hundred, hundred-fifty watt. But I'd seen better. Susan could have smiled her right into the woodwork. She moved her body slightly in the chair. She remained trim and upright, but somehow a wiggle came through.

I said, "If you bat your eyes at me I'm calling a policewoman."

She wiggled again, without moving. *How the hell does she do that?*

"I've got to trust you," she said. "I have no one else. I must turn to you."

"Hard," I said. "Hard for a woman alone, I'll bet."

Wiggle. Smile. Sigh. "Yes, I've got to find someone to help me. Will it be you?" She leaned forward slightly. She moistened her lower lip. "Will you help me?"

"I would gather stars," I said, "out of the blue."

"Don't make fun of me," she said. "I'm desperate."

"What are you desperate about?"

"My son. His father has taken him."

"And what would you like me to do?"

"Bring him back."

"Are you divorced?"

"Yes."

"Do you have custody?"

"Yes, of course. I'm his mother."

"Does his father have visitation privileges?"

"Yes, but this isn't a visit. He's taken Paul and he won't bring him back."

"And the court?"

"There's a hearing, and Mel's being subpoenaed but they can't find him."

"Is Mel your husband?"

"Yes. So I've spoken to the police and they said if they could find him they'd serve him a summons. But you know they aren't going to look for him."

"Probably not. They are sometimes busy," I said.

"And so I want you to find him and bring my Paul back."

"How's the boy feel about all this?"

"Naturally he wants to be with his mother, but he's only fifteen. He has no say. His father has simply taken him and hidden him."

"Mel misses Paul that much?"

"He doesn't miss him. He doesn't care about Paul one way or the other. It's merely his way of getting at me. He doesn't want me to have Paul."

"So he took him."

"Yes."

"Good deal for the kid," I said.

"Mel doesn't care about that. He wants to hurt me. And he's not going to."

There was no wiggle when she said the last sentence. "I want you to bring that kid back to me, away from his father. Paul is legally mine."

I was silent.

"I can pay any reasonable fee," she said. "I got an excellent alimony settlement." She was quite brisk and business-suity again.

I took in some air and let it out through my nose. I looked at her.

She looked back.

"What's the matter," she said.

I shook my head. "It does not sound like a real good time," I said.

"Mr. Spenser," the lower lip moistened again, mouth open a little, tip of the tongue running along the inner edge of the lip. "Please. I have no one else. Please."

"There's a question whether you need anyone else," I said, "but I'll take a whack at it on one condition."

"What?"

"You tell me your name so I'll know where the bill gets sent."

She smiled. "Giacomin," she said, "Patty Giacomin."

"Like the old Ranger's goalie," I said.

"I'm sorry?"

"Gentleman of the same name used to be a hockey player."

"Oh. I'm afraid I don't follow sports much."

"No shame to it," I said. "Matter of not being raised properly. Not your fault at all."

She smiled again, although this time it was a little unsure, as if now that she had me she wasn't certain she wanted me. It's a look I've seen a lot.

"Okay," I said. "Tell me everything you can think of about where old Mel might be."

I pulled a lined white pad closer, picked up a pencil, and listened.

CHAPTER 2

At 120,000 miles my 1968 Chevy convertible had bought the farm. There's just so much you can do with duct tape. With some of Huge Dixon's bounty money I had bought Susan's maroon MGB with whitewalls and a chrome luggage rack on the trunk lid, and at ten fifteen the next morning I was sitting in it outside an apartment building on Hammond Pond Parkway in Chestnut Hill. According to Patty Giacomin her husband's girl friend lived there. She knew that because she had once followed her husband out here and seen him go in and come out with a woman from his office named Elaine Brooks.

I'd asked how she knew it was a girl friend and not just business and Patty Giacomin had given me a look of such withering scorn that I'd let it go. Patty didn't know where her husband lived. She couldn't reach him through his office. They didn't know where he was. The girl friend was all we could think of.

"He'll show up there," Patty had said, "unless he's got a new one. He's always got to have a little honey."

So I sat with the motor idling and the heater on. The temperature had dropped forty-two degrees since yesterday and January in Boston was back to normal. I turned on the radio. A disc jockey with a voice like rancid lard was describing how much he liked the new record by Neil Diamond. Then Neil began to sing his new record. I shut it off.

A lot of cars went by heading under Route 9 for the Chestnut Hill Mall. There were two Bloomingdale's in Chestnut Hill Mall. Susan and I had come shopping there two weeks before Christmas, but she'd complained of sensory overload and we'd had to leave.

A jogger went by with a watch cap pulled over his ears and a blue jacket on that said TENNNESSEE TECH STAFF. Even in the cold his stride had an easy spring to it. I'd done the same thing along the Charles three hours earlier and the wind off the river had been hard as the Puritan God. I looked at my watch. Ten forty-five. I turned on the radio again and fished around until I found Tony Cennamo's jazz show. He was doing a segment on Sonny Rollins. I listened.

At eleven the show was over and I shut the radio off again. I opened my businesslike manila folder and looked at my page and a half of notes. Mel Giacomin was forty. He ran an insurance agency in Reading and until his divorce he had lived on Emerson Road in Lexington. His wife lived there still with their fifteen-year-old son, Paul. As far as his wife knew, the agency did well. He also ran a real estate business out of the same office and owned several apartment houses, mostly in Boston. The marriage had been troubled from the start, in dissolution for the last five years, and husband and wife had separated a year and a half ago. He'd moved out. She never knew where. The divorce proceedings had been bitter, and the decree had become final only three months ago.

Giacomin was, in his wife's phrase, "a whoremonger" and, his wife said, was very active among the younger women in his office and elsewhere. I looked at his picture. Long nose, small eyes, big droopy mustache. Hair worn medium length over the ears. On the back I read his wife's description: 6'1", 210-225 (weight varied depending on how much he was drinking and exercising and dieting). Had been a football player at Furman and still showed signs of it.

I had a picture of the boy too. He had his father's nose and small eyes. His face was narrow and sullen. His dark hair was long. His mouth was small and the upper lip formed a cupid's bow.

I looked again at my watch. Eleven thirty. He probably wasn't into morning sex. I didn't know what she looked like. There was no picture available and Patty Giacomin's description was sketchy. Blond hair in a curly perm, medium height, good figure. "Busty," Patty had said. I'd called Giacomin's office at nine, nine thirty, and ten of ten and she'd not been in. Neither had he. No one knew when to expect either. I looked at my watch again. Eleven thirty-five. I was sick of sitting. I pulled the MG up around the corner onto Heath Street and parked and walked back down to the apartment building. On the directory inside the outer doors Elaine Brooks was listed on the third floor, apartment 315. I pushed the buzzer. Nothing happened. I pushed it again and held it. After nearly a minute a thick female voice said hello through the intercom. The voice had been sleeping one minute prior.

I said, "Harry?"

She said, "What?"

I said, "Harry. It's me, Herb."

She said, "There's no goddamned Harry here."

I said, "What?"

She said. "You pushed the wrong button, you asshole."

I said, "Oh, sorry." The intercom went dead.

She was in there and I'd wakened her. She wouldn't be going right out. I went back and got into my car and drove the two or three hundred yards to Bloomingdale's and brought a big silver wine bucket for a hundred bucks. It left me two dollars for lunch. If I got a chance for lunch. I was hungry. But I was used to that. I was always hungry. I had the wine bucket gift wrapped and went back to the apartment building. I parked out front this time and went into the foyer and rang Elaine Brooks again. She answered the first buzz and her voice had freshened up some.

"Package for Ms. Brooks," I said.

"Just leave it in the foyer," she said. "I'll get it in a while."

"Mr. Giacomin said deliver it personal, ma'am. He said don't leave it in the hall or nothing. He said give it right to you."

"Okay," she said, "bring it up."

I said, "Yes, ma'am." The door buzzed and I went in. I was wearing off-white straight-legged Levi's cords, and moccasins and a blue wool shirt and a beige poplin jacket with a sheepskin lining and collar. A little slick for a cabbie maybe—if she noticed how much the shirt cost, but she probably wouldn't.

I took the elevator to the third floor and counted numbers to 15. I knocked. There was silence while I assume she peeped out through the little spyglass. Then the door opened on a safety chain and a narrow segment of face and one eye looked out at me. I'd figured on that. That's why I'd bought the bucket. In the box it was much too big to fit through a safety chain opening. I held the box up and looked at the small opening.

She said, "Okay, just a minute," and closed the door. I heard the chain slide off and then the door opened. The Bloomingdale's wrapper does it every time. Maybe I should rely on that more and on my smile less.

The door opened. She was as described only better looking. And she was busty. So is Dolly Parton. She'd done her hair and face, but hadn't dressed yet. She wore a long brown robe with white piping and a narrow white belt tied in front. Her feet were bare. Her toenails were painted. It didn't help much. Never saw a toenail I liked.

"Here you go, ma'am," I said.

She took the package. "Any message?"

"Not to me, ma'am. Maybe inside. All Mr. Giacomin told me was see that I put it right in your hands."

"Well, thank you," she said.

"Okay." I didn't move.

She looked at me. "Oh," she said. "Wait a minute." She closed the door and was gone maybe a minute and then the door opened and she gave me half a buck. I looked at it sort of glumly.

"Thanks," I said.

She closed the door without comment and I went on back down to the car. I pulled out of the turnaround in front of the apartment and parked up the road a little so I could see in the rearview mirror. And I waited.

I'd accomplished a couple of things maybe. One, for certain, I knew what she looked like so if she left I could follow; otherwise, I had to wait for old Mel to show up. The second thing, maybe, was she'd call to thank him for the gift and he'd say he never sent it and that would stir them up and one would go to the other. Or it would make them especially careful and I wouldn't be able to find him through her. The odds were with me though. And if his wife was right, he was too randy to stay away from her forever.

Over the years I'd found that stirring things up was better than not. When things got into motion I accomplished more. Or I seemed to.

CHAPTER 3

When she came out I almost missed her. I was watching the front door and just caught a glimpse of her as she cruised out from behind the apartment building in a black Buick Regal. I got in behind her, separated by one car as she swung up onto Route 9 and headed west. She had no reason to be looking for a tail and I had no reason to be tricky about it. I stayed a car or two behind her all the way onto 128 North and up Route 93 and onto Route 125 in Andover. Route 125 was harder. It was nearly deserted, running through the Harold Parker State Forest. Staying too close to her might make her notice. I hung a long way back and almost missed her again when she turned off just before Route 114 and went down Chestnut Street in Andover. What saved me was the red light. The car that had been ahead of her was stopped at it, and she wasn't there. She must have taken the left just before it. I yanked the MG around and accelerated down Chestnut Street. It was a winding back road at this end and the MG did much better time than the Buick. I caught sight of her in about two hundred yards. I slowed and let her pull ahead again. A mile or so farther and she stopped on the right-hand side. I turned right a block behind her and stopped out of sight and got out and walked back. Her car was there and she was disappearing into a big white house on the right.

I walked down. The house she was parked in front of was a two-family, up and down. The front hall door was unlocked and inside were two other doors. The one on the right obviously led to the downstairs apartment. The one directly ahead to the upstairs. I put my ear against the downstairs door. I could hear a TV set and the sound of a baby crying. That wouldn't be Giacomin. If she was visiting Giacomin. For all I knew she was here to play Parcheesi with an elderly aunt.

I tried the knob of the upstairs door. It turned but the door didn't open. Above it was the round key side of a spring bolt. They were easy, if the jamb wasn't tight. I took a thin plastic shim from my coat pocket and tried it. The jamb wasn't tight. I popped the bolt back and opened the door. The stairs rose straight up ahead of me to a landing and then they turned right. I went up them. At the top was another door. I put my ear against it. I could hear a radio and the low sound of conversation.

I put my hand on the knob and turned it quietly. The door was not locked. I opened it silently and stepped into a kind of foyer. Ahead was a dining room. To my right a living room through an archway. In the living room Elaine Brooks sat in a red plush armchair leaning forward, talking with a big man with a long nose and small eyes and a droopy mustache. *Elementary, my dear Watson, elementary.*

She didn't see me, her back was toward me. But he did. He was standing with a drink in his hand while she talked to him, and when I opened the door we looked right at each other. I had never figured the drill on a situation like this. Did I say "Ah, hah" vigorously, or just stare accusingly. He was quicker than I. He knew just the right thing to say.

He said, "What the hell do you want?"

"Perfect," I said. "The very phrase."

Elaine Brooks turned and looked at me. Her eyes widened.

"That's him, Mel," she said. "That's the guy brought the package from you."

Giacomin was wearing a gold Ban-Lon turtleneck and green polyester pants with no belt loops and one of those little flaps that buttons across in front instead of a belt. On the little finger of his right hand was a silver ring in the form of a snake biting its tail. On the little finger of his left hand was a silver ring with an amethyst set in it. The Ban-Lon shirt was not flattering to his body. He was fat around the middle. He said, "I asked you a question. I want an answer and I want it now."

I said, "You shouldn't wear a Ban-Lon shirt like that if you're going to scare people. It's a loser. Cary Grant wouldn't look good in Ban-Lon, you know."

"What did you bring her a present for? What the hell you doing trying to sneak into my house?"

I noticed he had sucked up his gut a little, but there's not a lot you can do with beer wings. I said, "My name is Spenser. I know it sounds corny, but I'm a private detective. Your wife hired me to find her son."

"My ex-wife," he said. "She offered to screw you yet?"

"No. I was surprised. Most women do at once." I looked at Elaine Brooks. "Am I starting to show my age, you think? I'm zero for two today."

Giacomin said, "Listen, Jack, I've heard all I'm going to hear from you. Move out."

I shook my head. "Nope. I need to stay and talk a little about your kid. Let's start over. Pretend I haven't snuck in here. Pretend you haven't yelled at me. Pretend I haven't been a wise guy. It's a bad habit, I know, but sometimes I can't resist."

"The kid ain't here. Now get the hell out of here or I'm going to throw you down the stairs."

"Now I told you, we have to talk. I am very stubborn. Maybe I've lost my sex appeal, but I'm still stubborn. I'm going to find that kid and I'm pretty sure you can help."

Giacomin was looking at me. He was a big guy and he'd played football, and he was probably used to being tough. But he probably also knew something about physical potential from his old football days and I think he had a suspicion that he couldn't throw me down the stairs.

"I don't know where he is," Giacomin said.

"Are you worried at all about the fact that his mother doesn't know either?" I said.

"She tell you that?" he said.

"Not exactly. She told me he was with you."

"Well, I told you before he's not. Now are you going to leave or am I going to call the cops?"

"You're going to call the cops," I said.

"You think I won't?"

"I think you won't," I said.

"You think you can stop me?"

"I don't need to. I don't want to. I enjoy meeting policemen. Sometimes if you're good they let you play with their handcuffs."

He looked at me. Elaine Brooks looked at me. If there'd been a mirror, I would have looked at me. But there wasn't. So I looked at them. In the quiet I could hear a television playing. It didn't seem to be from downstairs.

"Look, Jack, I'm getting pretty tired of you," he said. "What is it you want?"

"I want to take your kid back to his mother," I said. "I told you that already."

"And I told you he ain't here."

"Why don't I look around and prove it to myself," I said.

"You got a search warrant?"

"A search warrant? You gotta stop watching *Starsky and Hutch*," I said. "I'm not a cop. I don't get search warrants."

"You can't just walk in here and search my house," he said.

"Why not?"

We looked at each other some more. I was pretty sure the kid was there. If he wasn't, why not call the cops? All I had to do was stay there. They'd bend. They wouldn't be able to think of anything else to do.

Giacomin stopped looking at me long enough to look at his girl friend. She didn't have anything to offer. He looked back at me.

"All right," he said. "I've had enough. Either you walk out of here now or I kick your ass out."

"Don't do that," I said. "You're out of shape. I'll hurt you."

Giacomin looked at me and looked away. I knew he wasn't going to.

"The hell with it," he said with a small push-away hand gesture. "It's not worth a fight. Take him. He's down the hall." Giacomin gestured with his head. He didn't look at me or Elaine Brooks.

But the boy wasn't down the hall. He was right

around the corner in the dining room. He stepped into sight around the archway.

"Swell fight you put up for me, Daddy dear," he said.

He was a short thin kid and his voice had a soft whine to it. He was wearing a short-sleeved vertically striped dress shirt that gapped open near his navel, and maroon corduroy pants and Top-Siders with the rawhide lacing gone from one.

Giacomin said, "You remember who you're talking to, kid."

The kid smiled without humor. "I know," he said. "I know who I'm talking to, Dads."

Giacomin turned away from him and was silent.

I said, "My name is Spenser. Your mother sent me to bring you back to her."

The kid shrugged elaborately. I noticed that the pants were too big for him. The crotch sagged.

"You want to go?" I said.

He shrugged again.

"Would you rather stay here?"

"With him?" The kid's soft whine was full of distaste.

"With him," I said. "Or would you prefer to live with your mother?"

"I don't care."

"How about you?" I said to Giacomin. "You care?"

"The bitch got everything else," he said. "She can have him too. For now."

I said, "Okay, Paul. You got any stuff to pack?"

He shrugged. The all-purpose gesture. Maybe I should work on mine.

"He's got nothing to pack," Giacomin said. "Everything here is mine. She isn't getting any of it."

"Smart," I said. "Smart. I like a man gets out of a marriage gracefully."

"What the hell's that supposed to mean?" Giacomin said.

"You wouldn't know," I said. "The kid got a coat? It's about nineteen degrees out. I'll see that she sends it back if you want."

Giacomin said to his son, "Get your coat."

The boy went to the front hall closet and took out a navy pea coat. It was wrinkled, as if it had been crumpled on the floor rather than hanging. He put it on and left it unbuttoned. I opened the door to the stairs and he walked through it and started down the stairs. I looked at Giacomin.

"You've gotten yourself in a lot of trouble over this, Jack, and don't you forget it," he said.

I said, "Name's Spenser with an *S*, like the poet. I'm in the Boston book." I stepped through the door and closed it. Then I opened it again and stuck my head back into the hall. "Under Tough," I said. And closed the door, and walked out.

CHAPTER 4

The kid sat in the front seat beside me and stared out the window. His hands fidgeted on his lap. His fingernails were chewed short. He had hangnails. I turned left at the foot of Chestnut Street and drove south past the Academy.

I said, "Who would you rather live with, your mother or your father?"

The kid shrugged.

"Does that mean you don't know or you don't care?" I said.

"I don't know."

"Does that mean you don't know the answer to my question or you don't know who you'd rather live with?" I said.

The kid shrugged again. "Can I turn on the radio?" he said.

I said, "No. We're talking."

He shrugged.

"Would you rather be adopted?"

This time he didn't shrug.

"A ward of the state?"

Nothing.

"Join a gang of pickpockets and live in the slums of London?"

He looked at me as if I were crazy.

"Run off and join the circus? Make a raft and float down the Mississippi? Stow away on a pirate ship?"

"You're not funny," he said.

"Lot of people tell me that," I said. "Who would you rather live with, your mother or your father?"

"What'll you do if I won't say?" he said.

"Ride around and be funny at you till you plead for mercy."

He didn't say anything. But he didn't shrug. And he did look at me. Briefly.

"Want me to turn around and take you back to your father?"

"What difference does it make?" the kid said. "What do you care? It's not your business. Whyn't you leave me alone?"

"Because right now you're in my keeping and I'm trying to decide what's best to do with you."

"I thought my mother hired you. Whyn't you do what she tells you?"

"I might not approve of what she wants me to do."

"But she hired you," he said.

"She gave me a hundred bucks, one day's pay. If you don't want me to take you to her, I'll take you back to your old man, give her back her hundred."

"I bet you wouldn't," he said. He was staring out the window when he said it.

"Convince me you should be with him and I will."

"Okay, I'd rather be with him," the kid said. His face was still turned to the window.

"Why?" I said.

"See. I knew you wouldn't," he said. He turned his face toward me and he looked as if he'd won something.

"I didn't say I wouldn't," I said. "I asked for reasons. This is important stuff, choosing a parent. I'm not going to have you do it to win a bet."

He stared out the window again. We were in North Reading, still going south.

"See, Paul, what I'm trying to do is get you to decide what you'd like best to do. Are the questions too hard for you? You want to try watching my lips move?"

With his face still turned to the window the kid said, "I don't care who I live with. They both suck. It doesn't make any difference. They're both awful. I hate them."

The soft whine was a little shaky. As if he might cry.

"Son of a bitch," I said. "I hadn't thought of that."

Again he looked at me in an odd sort of triumph. "So now what are you going to do?"

I wanted to shrug and look out the window. I said, "I'll probably take you back to your mother and keep the hundred dollars."

"That's what I thought," the kid said.

"Would you rather I did something else?" I said.

He shrugged. We were through Reading Square almost to 128. "Can I turn on the radio now?" he said.

"No," I said. I knew I was being churlish, but the kid annoyed me. In his whiny, stubborn desperation he irritated the hell out of me. Mr. Warm. There's no such thing as a bad boy.

The kid almost smirked.

"You want to know why I'm taking you to your mother?" I said.

"To get the hundred bucks."

"Yeah. But it's more than a hundred bucks. It's a way of thinking about things."

The kid shrugged. If he did it enough, I would

stop the car and bang his head on the pavement. "When all your options are lousy," I said, "you try to choose the least lousy. Apparently you're equally bad off with your mother or your father. Apparently you don't care which place you're unhappy. If I take you back to your father you're unhappy and I get nothing. If I take you back to your mother you're unhappy and I get a hundred bucks. So I'm taking you back to your mother. You understand?"

"Sure, you want the hundred."

"It would be the same if it were a dime. It's a way to think about things. It's a way not to get shoved around by circumstances."

"And Mommy will give you money," he said. "Maybe you can fuck her." He checked me carefully, looking sideways at me as he said it, to see how shocked I'd be.

"Your father suggested the same thing," I said. "Your mom into sex, is she?"

The kid said, "I dunno."

"Or you figure I'm so irresistible that it's inevitable."

The kid shrugged. I figured I could take maybe two more shrugs before I stopped the car. "I don't want to talk about it," he said.

"Then you shouldn't have brought it up," I said.

He was silent.

I turned off of Route 28 onto Route 128 South, toward Lexington.

"I also think it's bad form to talk about your mother that way to a stranger."

"Why?"

"It's not done," I said.

The kid shrugged and stared out the window. He had one shrug left.

"If my father had started to fight with you, what would you do?"

"I'd have subdued him."

"How?"

"Depends how tough he is."

"He used to be a football player and he still lifts weights at the health club."

I shrugged. It was catching.

"Do you think you could beat him up?" he said.

"Oh, sure," I said. "He's a big strong guy, I guess, but I do this for a living. And I'm in better shape."

"Big deal," the kid said.

"I didn't bring it up," I said.

"I don't care about muscles," the kid said.

"Okay," I said.

"I suppose you think you're a big man, having muscles," the kid said.

"I think they are useful to me in what I do," I said.

"Well, I think they're ugly."

I took my hands off the wheel long enough to turn my palms up.

"How come you're a detective?" he said.

"Like the man said, because I can't sing or dance."

"It's an awful gross job to me," he said.

I made the same palms-up gesture. We were passing the Burlington Mall. "What exit do I take?" I said.

"Four and two-twenty-five toward Bedford," he said. "How come you want to do a gross job?"

"It lets me live life on my own terms," I said. "You sure you mean toward Bedford?"

"Yes. I'll show you," he said. And he did. We turned off toward Bedford, turned right, and right again and over an overpass back toward Lexington. Emerson Road was not far off the highway, a community of similar homes with a lot of wood and glass and some stone and brick. It was contemporary, but it worked okay in Lexington. I parked in the driveway out front and we got out. It was late afternoon and the wind had picked up. We leaned into it as we walked to his back door.

He opened it and went in without knocking and without any announcement.

CHAPTER 5

I rang the doorbell a long blast and followed him in.
It was a downstairs hall. There were two white hol-
low core doors on the left and a short stairway to the
right. On the wall before the stairway was a big Mon-
drian print in a chrome frame. Four steps up was the
living room. As I went up the stairs behind the kid
his mother came to the head of the stairs.

The kid said, "Here's a big treat, I'm home."

Patty Giacomin said, "Oh, Paul, I didn't expect
you so soon."

She was wearing a pink silk outfit—tapered pants
with a loose-fitting top. The top hung outside the
pants and was gathered at the waist by a gold belt.

I was standing two steps down behind Paul on the
stairs. There was a moment of silence. Then Patty
Giacomin said, "Well, come up, Mr. Spenser. Have a
drink. Paul, let Mr. Spenser get by."

I stepped into the living room. There were two
glasses and a pitcher that looked like martini on the
low glass coffee table in front of the couch. There was
a fire in the fireplace. There was Boursin cheese on a
small tray and a plate of crackers that looked like
little shredded-wheat biscuits. And on his feet, po-
litely, in front of the couch was the very embodiment
of contemporary elegance. He was probably my

height and slim as a weasel. He wore a subdued gray herringbone coat and vest with charcoal pants, a narrow pink tie, a pin collar, and black Gucci loafers. A pink-and-charcoal hankie spilled out of the breast pocket of his jacket. His hair was cut short and off the ears and he had a close-cropped beard and a mustache. Whether to see or be seen I had no way to tell, but he was also sporting a pair of pink-tinted aviator glasses with very thin black rims. The pink tie was shiny.

Patty Giacomin said, "Paul, you know Stephen. Stephen, this is Mr. Spenser. Stephen Court."

Stephen put out his hand. It was manicured and tanned. St. Thomas, no doubt. His handshake was firm without being strong. "Good to see you," he said.

He didn't say anything to Paul and Paul didn't look at him. Patty said, "Would you join us for a drink, Mr. Spenser?"

"Sure," I said. "Have any beer?"

"Oh, dear, I'm not sure," she said, "Paul, go look in the refrigerator and see if there's any beer."

Paul hadn't taken his coat off. He went over to the TV set in the bookcase and turned it on, set no channel, and sat down in a black Naugahyde armchair. The set warmed up and a *Brady Bunch* rerun came on. It was loud.

Patty Giacomin said, "Paul, for God's sake," and lowered the volume. While she did that I went into the kitchen on my right and found a can of Schlitz in the refrigerator. There were two more with it, and not much else. I went back into the living room with my beer. Stephen was sitting again, sipping his martini, his legs arranged so as not to ruin the crease in his pants. Patty was standing with her martini in hand.

"Did you have much trouble finding Paul, Mr. Spenser?"

"No," I said. "It was easy."

"Did you have trouble with his father?"

"No."

"Have some cheese and a cracker," she said. I took some. Boursin on a Triscuit isn't my favorite, but it had been a long time since breakfast. I washed it down with the beer. There was silence except for a now softened *Brady Bunch*.

Stephen took a small sip of his martini, leaned back slightly, brushed a tiny fleck of something from his left lapel, and said, "Tell me, Mr. Spenser, what do you do?" I heard an overtone of disdain, but I'm probably too sensitive.

"I'm a disc jockey at Régine's," I said. "Haven't I seen you there?"

Patty Giacomin spoke very quickly. "Mr. Spenser," she said, "could I ask you a really large favor?"

I nodded.

"I, well, I know you've already done so much bringing Paul back, but, well, it's just that it happened much sooner than I thought it would and Stephen and I have a dinner reservation. . . . Could you take Paul out maybe to McDonald's or someplace? I'll pay of course."

I looked at Paul. He was sitting, still with his coat on, staring at *The Brady Bunch*. Stephen said, "There's a rather decent Chinese restaurant in town, Szechuan and Mandarin cooking."

Patty Giacomin had taken her purse off the mantel and was rummaging in it. "Yes," she said. "The Yangtze River. Paul can show you. That's a good idea. Paul always likes to eat there." She took a twenty out of her purse and handed it to me. "Here," she said. "That should be enough. It's not very expensive."

I didn't take the twenty. I said to Paul, "You want to go?" and then I shrugged at the same time he did.

"What are you doing?" he said.

"Practicing my timing," I said. "Your shrug is so expressive I'm trying to develop one just like it. You want to go get something to eat?"

He started to shrug, stopped, and said, "I don't care."

"Well, I do," I said. "Come on. I'm starving."

Patty Giacomin still held the twenty out. I shook my head.

"You asked for a favor," I said. "You didn't offer to hire me. My treat."

"Oh, Spenser," she said, "don't be silly."

"Come on, kid," I said to Paul. "Let's go. I'll dazzle you with my knowledge of Oriental lore."

The kid shifted slightly. "Come on," I said. "I'm hungry as hell."

He got up. "What's the latest you'll be home," he said to his mother.

"I'll be home before twelve," she said.

Stephen said, "Good meeting you, Spenser. Good seeing you, Paul."

"Likewise I'm sure," I said. We went out.

When we were in the car again Paul said, "Why'd you do it?"

"What, agree to take you to dinner?"

"Yes."

"I felt bad for you," I said.

"How come?"

"Because you came home after being missing and no one seemed glad."

"I don't care."

"That's probably wise," I said. "If you can pull it off." I turned out of Emerson Road. "Which way?" I said.

"Left," he said.

"I don't think I could pull it off," I said.

"What?"

"Not caring," I said. "I think if I got sent off to eat with a stranger my first night home I'd be down about it."

"Well, I'm not," he said.

"Good," I said. "You want to eat in this Chinese place?"

"I don't care," he said.

We came to a cross street. "Which way?" I said.

"Left," he said.

"That the way to the Chinese restaurant?" I said.

"Yes."

"Good, we'll eat there."

We drove through Lexington, along dark streets that were mostly empty. It was a cold night. People were staying in. Lexington looks like you think it would. A lot of white colonial houses, many of them original. A lot of green shutters. A lot of bull's-eye glass and small, paned windows. We came into the center of town, the green on the right. The statue of the Minuteman motionless in the cold. No one was taking a picture of it.

"It's over there," Paul said, "around that square."

In the restaurant Paul said, "How come you wouldn't let her pay for it?"

"It didn't seem the right thing to do," I said.

"Why not? Why should you pay? She's got plenty of money."

"If we order careful," I said, "I can afford this."

The waiter came. I ordered a Beck's beer for me and a Coke for Paul. We looked at the menu.

"What can I have?" Paul said.

"Anything you want," I said. "I'm very successful."

We looked at the menu some more. The waiter brought the beer and the Coke. He stood with his pencil and paper poised. "You order?" he said.

"No," I said. "We're not ready."

"Okay," he said, and went away.

Paul said, "I don't know what to have."

I said, "What do you like?"

He said, "I don't know."

I nodded. "Yeah," I said, "somehow I had a sense you might say that."

He stared at the menu.

I said, "How about I order for both of us?"

"What if you order something I don't like?"

"Don't eat it."

"But I'm hungry."

"Then decide what you want."

He stared at the menu some more. The waiter wandered back. "You order?" he said.

I said, "Yes. We'll have two orders of Peking ravioli, the duck with plum sauce, the moo shu pork, and two bowls of white rice. And I'll have another beer and he'll have another Coke."

The waiter said, "Okay." He picked up the menus and went away.

Paul said, "I don't know if I'll like that stuff."

"We'll find out soon," I said.

"You gonna send my mother a bill?"

"For the meal?"

"Yes."

"No."

"I still don't see why you want to pay for my dinner."

"I'm not sure," I said. "It has to do with propriety."

The waiter came and plunked the ravioli on the table and two bottles of spiced oil.

"What's propriety?" Paul said.

"Appropriateness. Doing things right."

He looked at me without any expression.

"You want some raviolis?" I said.

"Just one," he said, "to try. They look gross."

"I thought you liked to eat here."

"My mother just said that. I never been here."

"Put some of the oil on it," I said. "Not much. It's sort of hot."

He cut his ravioli in two and ate half. He didn't say anything but he ate the other half. The waiter brought the rest of the food. We each ate four of the raviolis.

"You put the moo shu in one of these little pancakes, see, like this. Then you roll it up, like this. And you eat it."

"The pancake doesn't look like it's cooked," Paul said.

I ate some moo shu pork. He took a pancake and did as I'd showed him.

I said, "You want another Coke?"

He shook his head. I ordered another beer.

"You drink a lot?"

"No," I said. "Not as much as I'd like."

He speared a piece of duck with his fork and was trying to cut it on his plate.

"That's finger food," I said. "You don't have to use your knife and fork."

He kept on with the knife and fork. He didn't say

anything. I didn't say anything. We finished eating at seven fifteen. We arrived back at his house at seven thirty. I parked and got out of the car with him.

"I'm not afraid to go in alone," he said.

"Me either," I said. "But it's never any fun going into an empty house. I'll walk in with you."

"You don't need to," he said. "I'm alone a lot."

"Me too," I said.

We walked to the house together.

CHAPTER 6

It was Friday night, and Susan Silverman and I were at the Garden watching the Celtics and the Phoenix Suns play basketball. I was eating peanuts and drinking beer and explaining to Susan the fine points of going back door. I was having quite a good time. She was bored.

"You owe me for this," she said. She had barely sipped at a paper cup of beer in one hand. There was a lipstick half moon on the rim.

"They don't sell champagne by the paper cup here," I said.

"How about a Graves?"

"You want me to get beat up," I said. "Go up and ask if they sell a saucy little white Bordeaux?"

"Why is everyone cheering?" she said.

"Westphal just stuffed the ball backward over his head, didn't you see?"

"He's not even on the Celtics."

"No, but the fans appreciate the shot. Besides, he used to be."

"This is very boring," she said.

I offered my peanuts to her. She took two.

"Afterwards I'll let you kiss me," I said.

"I'm thinking better of the game," she said.

Cowens hit an outside shot.

"How come most of the players are black?" Susan said.

"Black man's game," I said. "Hawk says it's heritage. Says there were a lot of schoolyards in the jungle."

She smiled and sipped at the beer. She made a face. "How can you drink so much of this stuff?" she said.

"Practice," I said. "Years of practice."

Walter Davis hit a jump shot.

"What were you saying before about that boy you found Wednesday? What's his name?"

"Paul Giacomin," I said.

"Yes," Susan said. "You said you wanted to talk about him."

"But not while I'm watching the ball game."

"Can't you watch and talk at the same time? If you can't, go buy me something to read."

I shelled a peanut. "I don't know," I said. "It's just that I keep thinking about him. I feel bad for him."

"There's a surprise."

"That I feel bad for him?"

"You'd feel bad for Wile E. Coyote," Susan said.

Westphal hit a left-handed scoop shot. The Celtics were losing ground.

"The kid's a mess," I said. "He's skinny. He seems to have no capacity to decide anything. His only firm conviction is that both his parents suck."

"That's not so unusual a conviction for a fifteen-year-old kid," Susan said. She took another peanut.

"Yes, but in this case the kid may be right."

"Now you don't know that," Susan said. "You haven't had enough time with them to make any real judgment."

The Suns had scored eight straight points. The Celtics called time out.

"Better than you," I said. "I been with the kid. His clothes aren't right and they don't fit right. He doesn't know what to do in a restaurant. No one's ever taught him anything."

"Well, how important is it to know how to behave in a restaurant?" Susan said.

"By itself it's not important," I said. "It's just an instance, you know? I mean no one has taken any time with him. No one has told him anything, even easy stuff about dressing and eating out. He's been neglected. No one's told him how to act."

The Celtics put the ball in play from midcourt. Phoenix stole it and scored. I shook my head. Maybe if Cousy came out of retirement.

Susan said, "I haven't met this kid, but I have met a lot of kids. It is, after all, my line of work. You'd be surprised at how recalcitrant kids this age are about taking guidance from parents. They are working through the Oedipal phase, among other things, often they look and act as if they haven't had any care, even when they have. It's a way to rebel."

The Celtics threw the ball away. The Suns scored.

I said, "Are you familiar with the term blowout?"

"Is it like a burnout?" she said.

"No, I mean the game. You are witnessing a blowout," I said.

"Are the Celtics losing?"

"Yes."

"Want to leave?"

"No. It's not just who wins. I like to watch the way they play."

She said, "Mmm."

I got another bag of peanuts and another beer. With five minutes left the score was 114 to 90. I looked up at the rafters where the retired numbers hung.

"You should have seen it," I said to Susan.

"What?" She brushed a peanut shell from her lap. She was wearing blue jeans from France tucked into the tops of black boots.

"Cousy and Sharman, and Heinsohn and Lostcutoff and Russell. Havlicek, Sanders, Ramsey, Sam Jones, and K. C. Jones, Paul Silas and Don Nelson. And the war they'd have with the Knicks with Al McGuire on Cousy. And Russell against Chamberlain. You should have seen Bill Russell."

She said, "Yawn." The sleeves of her black wool turtleneck were pushed up on her forearms and the skin of her forearms was smooth and white in contrast. On a gold chain around her neck was a small diamond. She'd removed her engagement ring when she'd gotten divorced and had the stone reset. She'd had her hair permed into a very contemporary bunch of small Afro-looking curls. Her mouth was wide and her big dark eyes hinted at clandestine laughter.

"On the other hand," I said, "Russell ought to see you."

"Gimme a peanut," she said.

The final score was 130 to 101 and the Garden was nearly empty when the buzzer sounded. It was nine twenty-five. We put on our coats and moved toward the exits. It was easy. No pushing. No shoving. Most people had left a long time ago. In fact most people hadn't come at all.

"It's a fine thing that Walter Brown's not around to see this," I said. "In the Russell years you had to fight to get in and out."

"That sounds like a good time," Susan said. "Sorry I missed it."

On Causeway Street, under the elevated, it was very cold. I said, "You want to walk up to The Market? Or shall we go home?"

"It's cold," Susan said. "Let's go home to my house and I'll make us a goodie." She had the collar of her raccoon coat turned up so that her face was barely visible inside it.

The heater in my MG took hold on Route 93 and we were able to unbutton before we got to Medford. "The thing about that kid," I said, "is that he's like a hostage. His mother and father hate each other and use him to get even with each other."

Susan shook her head. "God, Spenser, how old are you? Of course they do that. Even parents who don't hate each other do that. Usually the kids survive it."

"This kid isn't going to survive it," I said. "He's too alone."

Susan was quiet.

"He hasn't got any strengths," I said. "He's not smart or strong or good-looking or funny or tough. All he's got is a kind of ratty meanness. It's not enough."

"So what do you think you'll do about it?" Susan said.

"Well, I'm not going to adopt him."

"How about a state agency. The Office for Children, say, or some such."

"They got enough trouble fighting for their share of federal funds. I wouldn't want to burden them with a kid."

"I know people who work in human services for the state," Susan said. "Some are very dedicated."

"And competent?"

"Some."

"You want to give me a percentage?"

"That are dedicated and competent?"

"Yeah."

"You win," she said.

We turned onto Route 128. "So what do you propose," Susan said.

"I propose to let him go down the tube," I said. "I can't think of anything to do about it."

"But it bothers you."

"Sure, it bothers me. But I'm used to that too. The world is full of people I can't save. I get used to that. I got used to it on the cops. Any cop does. You have to or you go down the tube too."

"I know," Susan said.

"On the other hand I may see the kid again."

"Professionally?"

"Yeah. The old man will take him again. She'll try to get him back. They're too stupid and too lousy to let this go. I wouldn't be surprised if she called me again."

"You'd be smart to say no if she does. You won't feel any better by getting into it again."

"I know," I said.

We were quiet. I turned off of Route 128 at the Smithfield Center exit and drove to Susan's house.

"I've got a bottle of new Beaujolais," Susan said in the kitchen. "How about I make us a couple of cheeseburgers and we can eat them and drink the Beaujolais?"

"Will you toast my hamburger roll?" I said.

"I certainly will," Susan said. "And who knows, maybe later I'll light your fire too, big fella."

"Oh, honeylips," I said. "You really know how to talk to a guy."

She handed me the bottle of wine. "You know where the corkscrew is," she said. "Open it and let it breathe a little, while I do the cheeseburgers."

I did.

CHAPTER 7

Patty Giacomin called me in April on a Tuesday afternoon at four o'clock. I hadn't heard from her in three months.

"Could you come to the house right now," she said.

I had been sitting in my office with my feet up on the desk and the window open sniffing the spring air and reading *A Distant Mirror* by Barbara Tuchman. I kept my finger in my place while I talked on the phone.

"I'm fairly busy," I said.

"You have to come," she said. "Please."

"Your husband got the kid again?"

"No. He's not my husband anymore. No. But Paul was almost hurt. Please, they might come back. Please, come now."

"You in danger?"

"No. I don't know. Maybe. You've got to come."

"Okay," I said. "If there's any danger, call the cops. I'll be there in half an hour."

I hung up and put my book down and headed for Lexington.

When I got there Patty Giacomin was standing in the front doorway looking out. She had on a white headband and a green silk shirt, a beige plaid skirt and tan Frye boots. Around her waist was a wide brown belt and her lipstick was glossy and nearly brown. Probably just got through scrubbing the tub.

I said, "The kid okay?"

She nodded. "Come in," she said. "Thank you for coming."

We went into the hall and up the three steps to the living room. Outside the picture window at the far end of the living room things were beginning to bloom.

"Would you like a drink?" she said.

"Same as last time," I said. "I'll take a beer if you have one."

She went to the kitchen and brought me back a can of Budweiser and a beer mug.

"I don't need the mug," I said. "I'd just as soon drink from the can."

Somewhere in the house there was a television set playing. It meant Paul was probably in residence.

Patty poured herself a glass of sherry. "Sit down," she said.

I sat on the couch. She sat across from me in an armchair and arranged her legs. I looked at her knees. She sipped her sherry. I drank some beer.

She said, "Was the traffic bad?"

I said, "Mrs. Giacomin, I galloped out here to your rescue. Don't sit around and talk at me about traffic conditions."

"I'm sorry. It's just that, well, now that you're here, I feel a little foolish. Maybe I overreacted." She sipped some more of her sherry. "But, dammit, someone did try to take Paul again."

"Your husband?"

"It wasn't him, but I'm sure he was behind it."

"What happened?"

"A strange man stopped Paul on his way home

from school and told him that his father wanted to see him. Paul wouldn't go with him, so the man got out of the car and started after him, but there was a policeman at the school crossing and when Paul ran back toward him the man got back into his car and drove away."

"And Paul came home."

"Yes."

"He didn't say anything to the cop."

"No."

"He didn't—I know it's corny, but I used to be a cop—get a license number, did he?"

"I don't think so. He didn't say anything about it."

"And he didn't know the man."

"No."

We were quiet. I finished the beer. She sipped some more sherry. I looked at her knees.

"Have you told the cops?" I said.

"No."

"You figure he had some friend of his try to pick the kid up? And the friend was overzealous?"

"I don't know," she said. There was a little thigh beginning to show along with the knees. "He knows some terrible people. In his business he knew some very thuggy-looking people. I'm sure it was one of them."

"Wide lapels? Dark shirts? White ties? Big hats?"

"I'm serious," she said. "I think he knew some people on the wrong side of the law. Maybe he was on the wrong side sometimes himself."

"Why do you think so?"

"Oh, I don't know, just a sense. The kind of people he was with. How secretive he sometimes was." She spread her hands. "Just a sense. Would you like another beer?"

"Sure."

She went to the kitchen and got me one and popped the top for me and brought it to me. Then she poured herself another glass of sherry.

"Do you have a plan?" I said.

She was standing now with her legs apart and one hand on her hip looking at me. *Vogue* magazine.

"A plan?"

"You know, for me. What do you want me to do?"

"I want you to stay here with us," she said.

"Damn," I said. "You're the fifth beautiful woman today to ask me that."

"I want you to guard Paul and, the truth, me too. I don't know what Mel might do."

"Are you suggesting that he's capable of anything?"

"Yes. He is. I know you're laughing at me, but you don't know him. I'm afraid."

She sat on the edge of the chair, her knees pressed together, her hands, one of them holding the sherry, were pressed together on top of her knees. She leaned forward toward me and moistened her bottom lip with the tip of her tongue. Vulnerable.

"You want me to move right in here and spend the night and all?"

She lowered her eyes. "Yes," she said.

"That's quite expensive. That means you pay me twenty-four hours a day."

"That's all right, I have money. I don't care. I need someone here."

"For how long?" I said.

She looked startled. "I don't know. I haven't thought about it."

"I can't stay here till the boy's twenty-one. Guarding is a temporary measure, you know. You'll have to find a better solution in the long run."

"I will," she said. "I will. But just for a little while. I'm frightened. Paul is frightened. We need a man here."

I looked past her and at the head of the stairs, in shadow, Paul stood listening. We looked at each other. Then he turned and disappeared. I looked back at his mother.

She raised her eyes. "Will you stay?" she said.

"Sure. I'll have to go home and pack a bag."

"We'll come with you," she said. She was smiling. "Paul and I will ride along. I'd love to see where you live anyway."

"Well, I've got a sports car. There's only room for two in it."

"We'll take my car," she said. "That way we'll be safe with you. And we can stop and get dinner on the way back. Or would you like a home-cooked meal? Poor man, you probably eat out all the time. Are you married? No, you're not, are you. I think I knew that." She called up the stairs. "Paul. Paul, come down. Mr. Spenser is going to stay with us." She drank the rest of her sherry.

"We can get a sandwich or something on the way," I said.

"No. When we get back I'll cook supper for you. No argument . . . Paul, come on, we're going to get some of Mr. Spenser's things so he can stay."

Paul came down the few steps from his bedroom to the living room. He had on a long-sleeved shirt with pastel flowers all over it, black corduroy pants, and the Top-Sider moccasins. If anything, he'd gotten thinner since January.

I nodded at him. He didn't say anything. His mother said, "Get your coat, we're going to drive Mr. Spenser home to get his suitcase."

Paul put on the same pea coat he'd had in January. There were two buttons missing. But it was too warm to button it anyway. We climbed into Patty Giacomin's stick-shift Audi Fox and cruised into Boston. We went into my apartment, where Paul sat down with his hands in the pockets of his pea coat and put on my television. His mother told me the apartment was beautiful and referred to it as a bachelor pad. She looked at Susan's picture on the bookcase and asked about her. She remarked that the kitchen was spotless. I put some extra clothes and a shaving kit and a box of .38 ammunition in my suitcase and said I was ready. Patty asked if I didn't get lonely living alone. I said sometimes I did. Paul stared at a rerun of *My Three Sons*. She said she supposed it was easier for a man, living alone. I said I wasn't sure that it was, but that I had friends and I was often busy. I didn't try to explain about Susan.

On the way back to Lexington we stopped at a Star Market and Patty Giacomin cashed a check at the courtesy booth and bought some groceries. Then we went back to her house and she cooked us dinner. Steak, peas, and baked potato, and a bottle of Portuguese rosé. Innovative.

After dinner Paul returned to the tube and Patty Giacomin cleared the table. I offered to help.

"Oh, no," she said. "You sit right there. It's a pleasure to wait on a man again."

I looked at my watch. It wasn't ten o'clock yet.

CHAPTER 8

The Giacomin house was on three levels. I had a room on the first. There was a lavatory with a shower across the hall from me. There was a family room with a Ping-Pong table next to me, and next to the lavatory across the hall was an office where Mel Giacomin had worked out of his house occasionally when he'd lived there. The next level was living room with a dining el and kitchen. The third level was a bathroom and three more bedrooms. Patty Giacomin slept up there and so did Paul.

The next morning I drove Paul to school at seven twenty-five. He didn't eat any breakfast. When we left, his mother was in the bathroom with the door closed. I delivered him right to the school door.

When he got out, I said, "What time does school get over?"

He said, "Five after two, I guess. I don't know exactly."

I said, "When it gets out, I'll be right here at this door. Don't come out another one. Don't go anywhere with anyone but me."

He nodded and walked into the school. I noticed his hair wasn't combed. I sat in the car and watched him until he was out of sight, then I turned and drove back to Emerson Road. Patty Giacomin was out of the bathroom, bathed and powdered and shiny with makeup. She had on a red apron with yellow flowers and underneath it a maroon silk blouse, white tapered pants, and white sandals. There was polish on her toenails. Coffee was perking in an electric pot, bacon was frying. Toast was in the toaster. The dining room table was set for two and the orange juice was all poured. There was jam out and butter on a plate.

"Sit down," she said. "Breakfast is almost ready."

"Paul doesn't know what he's missing, going off to school like that," I said.

"Oh, he never eats breakfast. Hates it. I'm glad actually. He's such a grouch in the morning. How do you like your eggs?"

"Over easy."

"Sit," she said. "It's almost ready."

I sat.

"Drink your orange juice," she said. "Don't wait. I'll sit right down in a minute."

I drank my orange juice. Frozen. The toast popped. Patty Giacomin put the four slices on a plate, put four more pieces of bread in to toast, and put the plate on the table.

I said, "You want me to butter it?"

"Yes, thank you."

I buttered the toast. Patty put four strips of bacon and two eggs, over easy, on my plate and put my plate in front of me. She served herself one egg and two strips of bacon. Then she sat down and drank her orange juice.

"This is very nice," I said.

"Well, if you're going to be stuck here with a woman and a kid, I felt you should at least be treated right."

I poured some coffee first into her cup and then mine.

"You men will have to rough it this weekend though," she said.

I ate a piece of bacon and a bite of egg.

"I'll be going away for the weekend," she said.

I nodded.

"I'm going to New York to visit friends."

I nodded again, and ate some more.

"I go down every month, go to the theater, to a museum exhibit. It's very stimulating."

"Yeah," I said. I finished up my eggs.

She ate a small bite of her egg. "Do you know New York, Mr. Spenser?"

"I know what everyone means when they say that. I know midtown Manhattan."

"Yes, I suppose that's true, isn't it. That is what we mean by New York when we go to visit." She drank some coffee.

"Who stayed with Paul before when you'd go? Pinkerton man?"

She smiled at me, "No, I hired a woman, Mrs. Travitz, normally. Sometimes Sally Washburn would come in. I always got someone."

"You think Paul will mind staying alone with me?" I said.

She looked a little startled, as if I'd asked a dumb question.

"Oh, no. Paul likes you. He understands that I have to get away. That I must find some fulfillment of my own. He realizes I can't just be a mother, as I couldn't just be a wife."

"Of course," I said.

"It's remarkable, I think, how long it took women to

realize the value and need of self-actualization," she said.

"Isn't that amazing," I said. "How long it took."

"Yes, New York is my safety valve in a sense."

"Get a chance to shop while you're there," I said.

She nodded. "Yes, usually I spend a day on Fifth Avenue."

"Ever take Paul?"

"Oh, God, no. He wouldn't have any fun and he'd just drag along. No, he'd spoil it. You don't have children, do you?"

"Nope."

She made a little snorting laugh. "You're lucky," she said. "Twice lucky, you're a man and you have no children."

"What about self-actualization and stuff?" I said.

"I meant it. I struggle for that. But what good is it for a single woman?"

"Why is being married so important?" I said.

"Because that's where the bucks are," she said. "And you know it."

"I'm not sure I know that, but I've never been married."

"You know what I mean. Men have the money. A woman needs a man to get it."

"I wonder if Gloria Steinem makes house calls," I said.

"Oh, that's crap," Patty Giacomin said. Her color was high. "You probably mouth the liberal line like everyone else around here, but you know what's reality all right. Men have the money and the power and if a woman wants some, she better get hold of a man."

I shrugged. I was beginning to see where Patty had picked up the habit.

"I know some folks who might argue with you," I said. "But I'm not one of them. I'm too busy counting my money and consolidating my power."

She smiled. "You do look quite powerful," she said. "Do you lift weights?"

"Sometimes," I said.

"I thought so. My husband, my ex-husband, used to."

"Not enough," I said.

"That's right, you've seen him, haven't you. He's gotten fat. But when we met he was really quite good-looking."

"You really think he'll make another try for Paul," I said.

"Absolutely," she said. "He's, he's . . ." She groped for words. "I don't know, he's like that. He has to get even. He can't stand to lose."

"Capture the flag," I said.

"Excuse me?"

I shook my head. "Just musing aloud."

"No, please tell me. You said something. Do you disapprove of me?"

"It's not my business to approve or disapprove," I said. "It's my business to see that your kid is okay."

"But you said something before. Please tell me."

"I said capture the flag. The kid's like a trophy you two are fighting for."

"Well, that son of a bitch is not going to get him," she said.

"That's right," I said.

"Why don't you take your coffee into the living room and read the paper," she said. "I'll clean up here."

I did.

She bustled about in her flowered apron and put

the dishes away in the dishwasher and swept the floor. When my breakfast had settled and I'd finished the paper I went to my room and changed and went out to run.

The winter was over. The weather was good and somewhere the voice of the turtle was probably being heard. What I heard were mostly sparrows. I jogged toward the center of town, feeling the spring sun press on my back. There was still an edge to the air. It had not yet softened into summer. But by a mile I had a pleasant sweat working and my legs felt strong and my muscles felt loose. There were other joggers out, mostly women this time of day. Probably looking for a man to grab so they could cut in on the money and power. Probably why Susan had latched on to me. Poor old Patty. She'd read all the stuff in *Cosmopolitan* and knew all the language of self-actualization, but all she really wanted was to get a man with money and power.

Ahead of me a young woman was jogging. She had on the top of a beige-and-blue warmup suit and blue shorts cut high. I slowed down to stay behind her and appraise her stride in the high-cut shorts. Women looked realer in the spring. Like this one. She hadn't had a chance to get this year's tan yet and her legs were white and vulnerable-looking. Good legs though. I wondered if I offered her money and power if she'd jog with me. She might. On the other hand she might accelerate and run off and I wouldn't be able to catch her. That would be humiliating. I picked up the pace and went past her. She had big gold hoop earrings on and she smiled a good-fellowship smile at me as I went past. I tried to look powerful and rich, but she didn't hurry to catch me.

I cruised down through Lexington Center past the

Minuteman and looped back in a wide circle to Emerson Road. It took about an hour and a quarter, which meant I'd done seven or eight miles. Patty's car was gone. I did some stretching, took a shower, and dressed. I heard Patty's car pull in. And when I went out, she was just breezing into the kitchen with some groceries.

"Hi," she said. "Want some lunch?"

"Are you after my money and power?" I said.

She looked quickly sideways at me. "Maybe," she said.

CHAPTER 9

On the weekend Paul improved his TV viewing average. Patty Giacomin had departed to self-actualize in New York. I had the living room and Paul stuck to his bedroom except to make a periodic trip to the kitchen to stare, often for minutes, into the refrigerator. He rarely ate anything. Looking into the refrigerator seemed merely something to do.

I had to stick with him, so I couldn't run or build some cabinets in Susan's house like I'd promised I would. I read most of the day about Enguerrand de Coucy and life in the fourteenth century. Saturday afternoon I watched a ball game on the tube. About six o'clock Saturday afternoon I yelled up the stairs to him.

"You want some supper?"

He didn't answer. I yelled again. He came to his bedroom door and said, "What?"

I said, "Do you want some supper?"

He said, "I don't care."

I said, "Well, I'll make some, I'm hungry. If you want some, let me know."

He went back into his room. I could hear the sounds of an old movie playing.

I went to the kitchen and investigated. There were some pork chops. I looked into the cupboard. There was rice. I found some pignolia nuts and some canned pineapple, and some garlic and a can of mandarin oranges. I checked the refrigerator again. There was some all-purpose cream. Heavy would have been better, but one makes do. There were also twelve cans of Schlitz that Patty Giacomin had laid in before she left. She hadn't asked. If she'd asked, I'd have ordered Beck's. But one makes do. I opened a can. I drank some. Perky with a nice finish, no trace of tannin.

I cut the eyes out of the pork chops and trimmed them. I threw the rest away. Patty Giacomin appeared not to have a mallet, so I pounded the pork medallions with the back of a butcher knife. I put a little oil into the skillet and heated it and put the pork in to brown. I drank the rest of my Schlitz and opened another can. When the meat was browned, I added a garlic clove. When that had softened, I added some juice from the pineapple and covered the pan. I made rice with chicken broth and pignolia nuts, thyme, parsley, and a bay leaf and cooked it in the oven. After about five minutes I took the top off the frying pan, let the pineapple juice cook down, added some cream, and let that cook down a little. Then I put in some pineapple chunks and a few mandarin orange segments, shut off the heat, and covered the pan to keep it warm. Then I set the kitchen table for two. I was on my fourth Schlitz when the rice was finished. I made a salad out of half a head of Bibb lettuce I found in the refrigerator and a dressing of oil and vinegar with mustard added and two cloves of garlic chopped up.

I put out two plates, served the pork and rice on each of them, poured a glass of milk for Paul, and carrying my beer can, went to the foot of the stairs.

I yelled, "Dinner," loud. Then I went back and sat down to eat.

I was halfway through dinner when Paul appeared. He didn't say anything. He pulled out the chair opposite me and sat down at the place I'd set.

"What's this?" he said.

"Pork, sauce, rice, salad," I said. I took a bite of meat and washed it down with a sip of beer. "And milk."

Paul nudged at the pork medallion with his fork. I ate some rice. He picked up a lettuce leaf from the salad bowl with his fingers and ate it.

I said, "What were you watching?"

He said, "Television."

I nodded. He nudged at the pork medallion again. Then he took a small forkful of rice and ate it.

I said, "What were you watching on the television?"

"Movie." He cut a piece off the pork and ate it.

I said, "What movie?"

"*Charlie Chan in Panama.*"

"Warner Oland or Sidney Toler?" I said.

"Sidney Toler." He reached into the salad bowl and took a forkful of salad and stuffed it into his mouth. I didn't say anything. He ate some pork and rice.

"You cook this?" he said.

"Yes."

"How'd you know how to do that?"

"I taught myself."

"Where'd you get the recipe?"

"I made it up."

He looked at me blankly.

"Well, I sort of made it up. I've eaten an awful lot of meals and some of them were in places where they serve food with sauces. I sort of figured out about sauces and things from that."

"You have this at a restaurant?"

"No. I made this up."

"I don't know how you can do that," he said.

"It's easy once you know that sauces are made in only a few different ways. One way is to reduce a liquid till it's syrupy and then add the cream. What you get is essentially pineapple-flavored cream, or wine-flavored cream, or beer-flavored cream, or whatever. Hell, you could do it with Coke, but who'd want to."

"My father never cooked," Paul said.

"Mine did," I said.

"He said girls cook."

"He was half right," I said.

"Huh?"

"Girls cook, so do boys. So do women, so do men. You know. He was only half right."

"Oh, yeah."

"What did you do for supper when your mother wasn't home?"

"The lady who took care of me cooked it."

"Your father ever take care of you?"

"No."

We were through eating. I cleared the table and put the dishes into the dishwasher. I'd already cleaned up the preparation dishes.

"Any dessert?" Paul said.

"No. You want to go out and get ice cream or something?"

"Okay."

"Where should we go," I said.

"Baskin-Robbins," he said. "It's downtown. Near where we ate that time."

"Okay," I said. "Let's go."

Paul had a large cone of Pralines 'n Cream. I had nothing.

On the ride home Paul said, "How come you didn't have any ice cream?"

"It's a trade-off I make," I said. "If I drink beer I don't eat dessert."

"Don't you ever do both?"

"No."

"Never?"

I deepened my voice and swelled up my chest as I drove. I said, "Man's gotta do what he's gotta do, boy."

It was dark, and I couldn't see well. I thought he almost smiled.

CHAPTER 10

It was almost the first day of May and I was still there. Every morning Patty Giacomin made me breakfast, every noon she made me lunch, every evening she made dinner. At first Paul ate dinner with us, but the last week he'd taken a tray to his room and Patty and I had been eating alone. Patty's idea of fancy was to put Cheez Whiz on the broccoli. I didn't mind that. I used to like the food in the army. What I minded was the growing sense of intimacy. Lately at dinner there was always wine. The wine was appropriate to the food: Blue Nun; Riunite, red, white, and rosé; a bottle of cold duck. I'd eat the eye of the round roast and sip the Lambrusco, and she'd chatter at me about her day, and talk about television, and repeat a joke she'd heard. I had begun to envy Paul. Nothing wrong with a tray in your room.

It was warm enough for the top down when I dropped Paul off at school on a Thursday morning and headed back to Emerson Road. The sun was strong, the wind was soft, I had a Sarah Vaughan tape on at top volume. She was singing "Thanks for the Memories" and I should have been feeling like a brass band. I didn't, I felt like a nightingale without a song to sing. It wasn't spring fever. It was captivity.

While I could get in my miles every morning, I

hadn't been to a gym in more than two weeks. I hadn't seen Susan in that time. I hadn't been thirty-five feet from a Giacomin since I'd come out to Lexington. I needed to punch a bag, I needed to bench press a barbell, I needed very much to see Susan. I felt cramped and irritable and scratchy with annoyance as I pulled into the driveway.

There were flowers on the kitchen table, and places set for two, with a glass of orange juice poured at each place. And the percolator working on the counter. But Patty Giacomin wasn't in the kitchen. No eggs were cooking. No bacon. Good. My cholesterol count was probably being measured in light-years by now. I picked up one of the glasses of orange juice and drank it. I put the empty glass into the dishwasher.

Patty Giacomin called from the living room, "Is that you?"

"Yes, it is," I said.

"Come in here," she said. "I want your opinion on something."

I went into the living room. She was standing at the far end, in front of the big picture window that opened out onto her backyard. The morning sun spilled through it and backlit her sort of dramatically.

"What do you think?" she said.

She was wearing a metallic blue peignoir and was standing in a model's pose, one foot turned out at right angles, her knees slightly forward, her shoulders back so her breasts stuck out. The sunlight was bright enough and the robe was thin enough so that I was pretty sure she had nothing on under it.

I said, "Jesus Christ."

She said, "You like?"

I said, "You need a rose in your teeth."

She frowned. "Don't you like my robe," she said. Her lower lip pushed out slightly. She turned as she talked and faced me, her legs apart, her hands on her hips, the bright sun silhouetting her through the cloth.

"Yeah. The robe's nice," I said. I felt a little feverish. I cleared my throat.

"Why don't you come over and take a closer look?" she said.

"I can see an awful lot from here," I said.

"Wouldn't you like to see more," she said .

I shook my head.

She smiled carefully, and let the robe fall open. It hung straight and framed her naked body. The blue went nicely with her skin color.

"Are you sure you wouldn't like a closer look?" she said.

I said, "Jesus Christ, who writes your dialogue."

Her face flattened out.

"What?"

"This is how it would happen on *The Dating Game,* if they were allowed to film it."

She blushed. The robe hanging open made her seem less sexy than vulnerable.

"You don't want me," she said in a loud whisper.

"Sure, I want you. I want every good-looking woman I ever see. And when they point their pubic bone at me I get positively turbulent. But this ain't the way, babe."

Her face stayed flushed. Her voice stayed in the whisper, though it sounded hoarser and less stagey now.

"Why?" she said. "Why isn't it?"

"Well, for one thing, it's contrived."

"Contrived?"

"Yeah, like you read *The Total Woman* and took notes."

Her eyes had begun to fill. She had let her hands drop to her sides.

"And there's other things. There's Paul, for instance. And a woman I know."

"Paul? What the hell has Paul got to do with it?" She wasn't whispering now. Her voice was harsh. "I have to get Paul's permission to fuck?"

"It's not a matter of permission. Paul wouldn't like it if he found out."

"What do you know about my son?" she said. "What do you think he cares? Do you think he'd think less of me than he does now?"

"No," I said. "He'd think less of me."

She stood without movement for maybe five seconds. Then she deliberately took hold of her robe and shrugged it back over her shoulders and let it drop to the floor. She was naked except for a pair of sling-back pumps made of, apparently, transparent plastic. "You saw most of it already," she said. "Want to see it all?" She turned slowly around, 360 degrees, her arms out from her sides. "What do you like best?" she said. Her voice was very harsh now and there were tears on her cheeks. "You want to pay me?" She walked over to me. "You figure I'm a whore, maybe you'll pay me. Twenty bucks, mister? I'll give you a good time."

"Stop it," I said.

"Who'd tell Paul that you fucked his whorey mother? How would he find out you'd been dirty?"

Her voice was shaking and clogged. She was crying.

"You'd tell him when there was a good occasion. Or you'd tell his father and his father would tell him. And besides there's this woman I know."

Patty Giacomin pressed against me. Her shoulders were heaving, she was crying outright. "Please," she said. "Please. I've been good. I've cooked. I pay you. Please, don't do this."

I put my arms around her and patted her bare back. She buried her face against my chest and with both hands straight at her sides, stark naked except for her transparent shoes, she sobbed without control for a long time. I patted her back and tried to think of other things. *Carl Hubbell struck out Cronin, Ruth, Gehrig, Simmons, and Jimmy Foxx in an all-star game. Was it 1934?* The crying seemed to feed on itself. It seemed to build. I rested my chin on the top of her head. *Who played with Cousy at Holy Cross? Kaftan. Joe Mullaney? Dermie O'Connell. Frank Oftring.* Her body pressed at me. I thought harder: *All-time all-star team players I'd seen. Musial; Jackie Robinson; Reese; and Brooks Robinson. Williams; DiMaggio; Mays; Roy Campanella; Sandy Koufax, left-hand pitcher; Bob Gibson, right-hand pitcher; Joe Page in the bullpen.* She was crying easier now.

"Come on," I said. "You get dressed, I'll take a cold shower, and we'll have some breakfast."

She didn't move, but the crying stopped. I stopped patting. She stepped away and squatted gracefully to pick up the peignoir. She didn't put it on. She didn't look at me. She walked away toward her bedroom.

I went into the kitchen and stood at the open back door and took in a lot of late April air. Then I poured a cup of coffee and drank some and scalded my tongue a little. The principal of counterirritant.

It was maybe fifteen minutes before she came out of the bedroom. In the meantime I rummaged around in the kitchen and got together a potato-and-onion omelet. It was cooking when she came into the kitchen. Her makeup was good and her hair was neat, but her face still had the red, ugly look faces have after crying.

"Sit down," I said. "My treat this morning." I poured her coffee.

She sat and sipped at the coffee.

I said, "This is awkward, but it doesn't have to be too awkward. I'm flattered that you offered. You should not consider it a negative on you that I declined."

She sipped more coffee, shook her head slightly, didn't talk.

"Look," I said. "You've been through a lousy divorce. For sixteen years or more you've been a housewife and now all of a sudden there's no man in the house. You're a little lost. And then I move in. You start cooking for me. Putting flowers on the table. Pretty soon you're a housewife again. This morning had to happen. You had to prove your housewifery, you know? It would have been a kind of confirmation. And it would have confirmed a status that I don't want, and you don't really want. I'm committed to another woman. I'm committed to protecting your son. Screwing his mom, pleasant as that would be, is not productive."

"Why not?" She looked up when she said it and straight at me.

"For one thing it might eventually raise the question of whether I was being paid for protecting Paul or screwing you, of being your husband substitute."

"Gigolo?"

"You ought to stop doing that. Classifying things under some kind of neat title. You're a whore, I'm a gigolo, that sort of thing."

"Well, what was I if I wasn't a whore?"

"A good-looking woman, with a need to be loved, expressing that need. It's not your fault that you expressed it to the wrong guy."

"Well. I'm sorry for it. It was embarrassing. I was like some uneducated ginzo."

"I don't know that the lower classes do that sort of thing much more often than we upper-class types. But it wasn't simply embarrassing. It was also in some ways very nice. I mean I'm very glad to have seen you with your clothes off. That's a pleasure."

"I need men," she said.

I nodded. "That's where the bucks are," I said.

"That's still true," she said. "But it's more than that."

I nodded again.

"Women are so goddamned boring," she said. She stretched out the *or* in boring.

"Sometime I'll put you in touch with a woman I know named Rachel Wallace," I said.

"The writer?"

"Yeah."

"You know her? The feminist writer? Well, that's all right in theory. But we both know the reality."

"Which is?"

"That we get a lot further batting our eyes and wiggling our butts."

"Yeah," I said. "Look where it got you."

With a quick sweep of her right hand she knocked the half-full cup of coffee and its saucer off the table and onto the floor. In the same motion she got up out of her chair and left the kitchen. I heard her go up the short stairs to her bedroom and slam the door. She never did try my potato-and-onion omelet. I threw it away.

CHAPTER 11

It was two days after the peignoir that they came for the kid. It was in the evening. After supper. Patty Giacomin answered the doorbell and they came in, pushing her backward as they came. Paul was in his room watching television. I was reading *A Distant Mirror,* chapter seven. I stood up.

There were two of them and neither was Mel Giacomin. The one doing the shoving was short and dumpy and barrel-bodied. He was wearing the ugliest wig I've ever seen. It looked like an auburn Dynel ski cap that he'd pulled down over his ears. His partner was taller and not as bulky. He had a boot camp crew cut and a navy watch cap rolled up so that it looked like a sloppy yarmulke.

The short one said, "Where's the kid?"

The tall one looked at me and said, "Spenser. Nobody told me about you in this."

I said, "How are you, Buddy?"

The short one said, "Who's he?"

Buddy said, "He's a private cop. Name's Spenser. You working, Spenser?"

I said, "Yes."

"They didn't tell me you'd be here."

"Mel didn't know, Buddy. It's not Mel's fault."

"I didn't say anything about no Mel," Buddy said.

"Aw, come on, Buddy, don't be a jerk. Who the hell else would send you for the kid?"

The short one said, "Never mind all the crap. Parade the fucking kid out here."

I said to Buddy, "Who's your friend with his head in a bag?"

Buddy made a very small smile.

The short one said, "What the hell's that remark supposed to mean, douchebag?"

"It means you look like you're wearing an Astro-turf bathing cap for a rug. Funniest looking rug I've ever seen."

"Keep running your mouth, douchebag, and we'll see how funny you are."

Buddy said, "Be cool, Harold." To me he said, "We come to take the kid back to his old man. We didn't know you'd be here, but that don't change the plan."

I said, "No."

"No, we can't take him back? Or no, it don't change the plan," Buddy said.

"No, you can't take him back," I said.

Harold pulled a black woven leather sap from his hip pocket and tapped it gently against the palm of his hand.

"I'll enjoy this," he said. And I hit him a stiff left jab on his nose, turning my body sideways as I threw the punch to get all of me into it and to make a smaller target. The blood spurted out of Harold's nose and he staggered three steps backward, flailing his arms for balance. The blackjack hit a table lamp and smashed it. Harold got his balance. He held one hand against the blood coming from his nose and shook his head once as if there were a fly in his ear.

Buddy shrugged a little sadly. Harold came back at me and I hit him the same jab, same place, a little harder. It sat him down. Blood was all over his face and shirt.

"Jesus Christ, Buddy," he said. "Jump in. He can't take two of us."

"Yeah, he can," Buddy said. Harold started to get up. His legs were wobbly. Buddy said, "Leave it alone, Harold. He'll kill you if you try again."

Harold was on his feet, trying to keep his nose from bleeding. He still held the blackjack in his right hand, but he didn't seem to remember that. He looked confused.

I said, "That's what you brought for muscle, Buddy?"

Buddy shrugged. "He'd have been all right for the broad," he said. "He does good with barbers and car salesmen that get a little behind on the vig." Buddy spread his hands.

"How come Mel didn't come himself?"

"I don't know no Mel."

"Come on, Buddy. You want to discuss unlawful entry and assault with the Lexington cops?"

"What are they going to do, beat the shit out of me with a Minuteman?"

"Jail is jail is jail, babe. Don't matter who put you there. How long since you and Harold summered at Walpole?"

"How about we just walk out of here," Harold said. His voice was thick. He had a handkerchief wadded against his nose.

I reached around and took my gun out of its hip holster. I showed it to both of them. I smiled.

Buddy said, "So we know Mel. We thought we'd do him a favor. He heard that his old lady had hired some private cop to be a bodyguard. We figured we come get the kid for him. We didn't know it was you.

We figured it would be some stiff that used to be a bank guard. Hell, we didn't even bring a piece."

"How you happen to know Mel, Buddy?"

Buddy shrugged again. "Seen him around, you know. Just trying to do him a favor."

"What did he pay you?"

"A C each."

"Big league," I said.

"See you again," Buddy said. "Come on, Harold. We're walking."

Harold looked at the gun. He looked at Buddy. Buddy said, "Come on," and turned toward the front door. Harold looked at me again. Then he turned after Buddy.

Patty said, "Spenser."

I shook my head and put the gun away. "Tell Mel that if he keeps sending people down to annoy us I'm going to get mad," I said. Buddy nodded and went down the three stairs to the front hall. Harold followed him.

"The next people he sends won't walk out," I said.

Buddy paused and looked back. "You never were a shooter," he said. "It's what's wrong with you." Then he went out the front door and Harold went after him. I heard it close behind them.

Patty Giacomin stood where she'd stood throughout. "Why did you let them go?" she said.

"We had a deal," I said. "If they told me what I asked I wouldn't turn them in."

"You didn't say that," she said.

"Yeah, but Buddy and I both knew it."

"How do you know him? Who are they?"

"I don't know Harold. Buddy I've run into over the years. He works on the docks, and he grifts. He unloads ships when there's work. When there isn't, he steals. He's an errand boy. You want your warehouse burned for insurance, you give Buddy a couple of bucks and he torches it. You want a Mercedes sedan, you pay Buddy and he steals you one. Some grocery clerk owes you money and he won't pay and Buddy goes over and collects. Nothing heavy. Nothing complicated."

"He belongs in jail," Patty said.

"Yeah, I suppose so. He's been there. He'll be there again. He's not that bad a guy."

"Well, I think he's pretty bad," she said. "He broke into my house, manhandled me, tried to kidnap my son. I think he is very bad."

"Yeah, I suppose you would. But that's because you don't know any people who are in fact very bad."

"And you do?"

"Oh, my, yes," I said.

"Well, I'm glad I don't. I hope Paul didn't see this."

"Oh, he saw it," I said. I nodded at the stairs. In the shadows of the upper hall, three stairs up from the living room, Paul was standing looking down.

"Paul," she said. "How long have you been there?"

He didn't say anything.

I said, "Since Buddy and Harold came in."

"Don't be scared, Paul," she said. "It's okay, Mr. Spenser has made them go away. He won't let them bother us."

Paul came down the stairs and stood on the middle step.

"How come you didn't shoot them?" he said.

"I didn't need to," I said.

"Were you scared to?"

Patty Giacomin said, "Paul."

"Were you?"

"No."

"The guy said that there was something wrong with you. That you weren't a shooter."

"True."

"What'd he mean?"

Patty said, "Paul, that's enough. I mean it. You're being very rude."

I shook my head. "No. This all revolves around him. He has a right to ask questions."

"What did he mean?" Paul said.

"He meant that if I was quicker to kill people, my threat would work better."

"Would it?"

"Probably."

"Why don't you?"

"Something to do with the sanctity of life. That kind of stuff."

"Have you ever killed someone?"

Patty said, "Paul!"

"Yes."

"So?"

"I had to. I don't if I don't have to. Nothing's absolute."

"What do you mean?" He stepped down to the living room level into the light.

"I mean you make rules for yourself and know that you'll have to break them because they won't always work."

Patty said, "I don't know what either one of you is talking about, but I want you to stop. I don't want any more talking about killing and I don't want to talk about either of those men again. I mean it. I want it stopped." She clapped her hands when she said the last sentence. Paul looked at her as if she were a cockroach and turned and went back up to his room.

"I think I need a drink," Patty said. "Could you put one together for me?"

"Sure," I said. "What'll it be?"

CHAPTER 12

The next time they tried, it was meaner. Patty Giacomin was food shopping when I went to pick up Paul at school. When I came back into the house with Paul, the phone was ringing. Paul answered and then handed it to me.

"It's for you," he said.

I took the phone and Paul lingered in the doorway between the kitchen and the living room to see who it was. It was a voice I didn't know.

It said, "Spenser?"

I said, "Yeah."

It said, "There's someone here wants to talk with you."

I said, "Okay." Repartee is my game.

There was a shuffling at the other end, then Patty Giacomin's voice came on. It sounded shaky.

"Spenser. That man Buddy and some other men have me. They said if you don't give Paul to them they won't let me go."

I said, "Okay, put Buddy on. We'll work something out."

She said, "Spenser . . ." and then Buddy's voice came on.

"You there?"

I said, "Yeah."

Buddy said, "Here's the plan. You bring the kid to the Boston end of the Mass. Ave. Bridge. We'll bring Momma to the Cambridge end. When we see you start the kid we'll start Momma the other way. Get the idea?"

"Yeah. Shall we do it now?"

"One hour. We'll be there in one hour."

"Okay."

"Spenser?"

"Yeah?"

"Don't fuck this up. I got people with me that ain't Harold, you understand?"

"Yeah."

Buddy hung up.

I broke the connection and dialed information.

"Harbour Health Club in Boston," I said to the operator. I looked at my watch. Two twenty-five. The operator gave me the number. I punched it out on the push-button phone. It rang. A woman answered.

I said, "Henry Cimoli, please."

The woman said, "One minute." She sounded like she was chewing gum.

Henry said, "Hello."

I said, "Spenser. I need Hawk. You know where he is?"

Henry said, "I'm looking at him." Sometimes it's better to be lucky than good.

I said, "Put him on."

In a moment Hawk said, "Umm," into the phone.

I said, "You know Buddy Hartman?"

Hawk said, "Umm-hmm."

I said, "He and several others have a woman. They want to exchange her for a boy that I have. At three twenty-five they are going to be at the Cambridge end of the Mass. Ave. Bridge. I'm going to be at the Boston end. We're going to start them together. When they meet, halfway across, I want you to discourage Buddy and his pals while I drive out onto the bridge and pick up both of them, the woman and the kid."

Hawk said, "It's five minutes' work, but I gotta drive there and go home again. Cost you a deuce."

"Yeah, I haven't got time to haggle fee with you. I'm on my way."

"I be there," Hawk said. We hung up.

Paul was staring at me.

I said, "Come on, we gotta go get your mother."

"You going to give me to them?"

"No."

"What if they try to shoot me?"

"They won't. Come on. We'll talk in the car."

In the car I said, "You heard what I said on the phone to Hawk?"

Paul said, "Who's Hawk?"

"Friend of mine, doesn't matter. You heard what I said?"

"Yes."

"Okay. I can't believe we're talking a lot of danger here. But here's what I want you to do. When I tell you to go, you start walking along the Mass. Ave. Bridge toward Cambridge."

"Where's the Mass. Ave. Bridge?"

"Across the Charles, by MIT. You'll see. When your mother reaches you, say to her, 'Lie flat on the ground, Spenser's coming,' and then you drop flat down on the pavement. If she doesn't get down, tell her to. I'll drive out onto the bridge and I'll get out of the car. Tell her to get in the driver's side. You get in the other side."

"What about that Buddy?"

"Hawk will look after him till I get there."

"But what if he doesn't?"

I smiled. "You say that because you don't know Hawk. Hawk will take care of the Cambridge end." I wrote Susan's address on a piece of paper. "Have your mother drive you there."

The kid was nervous. He yawned repeatedly. I could hear him swallow. His face looked tight and without color. "What if she's not there?" he said.

"No reason she shouldn't be," I said.

"What if this doesn't work?"

"I'll make it work," I said. "I'm good at this. Trust me."

"What would they do if they got me?"

"Take you to your father. You wouldn't be any worse off than now. Relax. You got nothing to lose here. Your father wouldn't hurt you."

"He might," Paul said. "He doesn't like me. He just wants to get even with my mother."

I said, "Look, kid, there's just so much value to thinking about things you can't control. It's time to stop now. You've had a tough life and it doesn't seem to be looking up. It's time to start growing up. It's time to stop talking and start being ready. You know?"

"Ready for what?"

"For whatever comes along. Your way out of a lousy family life is to grow up early and you may as well start now."

"What am I supposed to do?"

"What I tell you. And do it with as little whining as you can. That would be a start."

"But I'm scared," Paul said. There was outrage in his voice.

"That's a normal condition," I said. "But it doesn't change anything."

He was silent. We passed Mount Auburn Hospital and crossed the Charles onto Soldier's Field Road. To the right Harvard Stadium looked like it was supposed to, round and looming with arches and ivy on the walls. The Harvard athletic plant sprawled for acres around it. Soldier's Field Road became Storrow Drive and I went off Storrow by BU, and made the complicated loop turn till I was heading inbound on Commonwealth. At Mass. Ave. there was an underpass. I stayed to the right of it and turned onto Mass. Ave. and drove past the up ramp from Storrow and parked on the bridge with my emergency lights blinking. It was three twenty. Beside me Paul's stomach rolled. He belched softly.

"You see them?" he said.

"No."

A car behind me blew its horn at me, and the driver glared as he went by. Two kids in a Buick pulled around the car. The one in the driver's seat gave me the finger. The passenger called me an asshole through his rolled-down window. I kept my eyes fixed on the Cambridge side of the bridge.

At three twenty-five I said to Paul, "Okay. It's time for you to walk. Tell me what you're going to do."

"I'm going to walk to the middle and when my mother gets to me I'm going to tell her lie down, that you're coming, and then I will lie down too."

"And if she doesn't hit the sidewalk?" I said.

"I'll tell her again."

"And when I show up what happens?"

"I get in one side. She gets in the other. We drive to that address."

"Good. Okay, walk across the street. They'll start her on their side."

He sat for a moment. Belched again. Yawned.

Then he opened the door of the MG and stepped out onto the sidewalk. He crossed and began to walk slowly toward the Cambridge side. He went about ten feet and looked back at me. I grinned at him and made a V with my fingers. He kept going. At the far end of the bridge I saw his mother get out of a black Oldsmobile and start toward us.

The Mass. Ave. Bridge is open. It rests on arches that rest on pilings. There's no superstructure. On a summer evening it is particularly pleasant for strolling across. It is said that some MIT students once measured it by repeatedly placing an undergraduate named Smoot on the ground and marking off his length. Every six feet or so there is still the indication of one smoot, two smoots, painted on the pavement. I could never remember how many smoots long the bridge was.

He was almost to his mother. Then they met. Across the bridge the Oldsmobile began to move, slowly. The boy dropped to the pavement. His mother hesitated and then crouched down beside him, tucking her skirt under her. *Flat,* I muttered, *flat, goddammit.*

I slammed the MG into gear and headed for Paul and his mother. Across the way the Olds began to pick up speed. A Ford station wagon swung around the corner from Memorial Drive, looped out into the wrong lane with a lot of squealing rubber and blaring horns, and rammed the Olds from the side, bouncing it against the high curb and pinning it. Before the cars had stopped, Hawk rolled out of the driver's side with a handgun the size of a hockey stick and took aim over the hood of the wagon. I cut across the traffic and rolled the MG up beside the sidewalk between the Olds and the two Giacomins.

From down the bridge I heard gunfire. I jerked up the emergency, slapped the car into neutral, and scrambled out of the MG.

"Patty, get in, take Paul and drive to Smithfield, Paul's got the address. Explain who you are and wait for me there. Move."

There was another gunshot from five smoots away. I had my gun out and was running toward the Olds when I heard the MG take off with its tires squealing. I was almost at the Olds when I saw Hawk go over the hood of the wagon, reach into the driver's side of the Olds and pull somebody out through the window with his left hand. With the barrel of his gun he chopped the pistol out of the other man's hand, shifted his weight slightly, put his right hand, gun and all, into the man's crotch and pitched him over the railing and into the Charles River.

A big guy with a tweed cap got out of the back seat of the Olds as I came around behind it. I turned sideways on my left foot and kicked him in the small of the back with my right. He sprawled forward and a gun that looked like a Beretta clattered on the pavement ahead of him as he sprawled. It skittered between the risers of the railing and into the river. I looked into the car and saw Buddy crouched down on the passenger's side of the front floorboards, huddled under the dash. Hawk looked in at the other window, the enormous handgun leveled. We saw Buddy at the same time.

Hawk said, "Shit," stringing out the vowel the way he did. From the Boston side of the bridge I heard a siren. So did Hawk. He put the bazooka away inside his coat.

"Let's split," I said.

He nodded. We ran down Mass. Ave. and into one of the MIT buildings.

We moved through a crowded corridor lined with ship models in glass cases.

"Try and look like an upwardly mobile nineteen-year-old scientist," I said.

"I am, bawse. I got a doctor of scuffle degree."

Hawk was wearing skintight unfaded jeans tucked into his black boots. He had on a black silk shirt unbuttoned nearly to his waist, and the handgun was hidden under a white leather vest with a high collar that Hawk wore turned up. His head was shaven and gleamed like black porcelain. He was my height, maybe a hair taller, and there was no flesh on his body, only muscle over bone, in hard planes. The black eyes over the high cheekbones were humorous and without mercy.

We went out a side door at the end of the corridor. Behind us there were still sirens. We strolled across the MIT campus away from Mass. Ave.

"Sorry about your car," I said.

"Ain't my car, man," Hawk said.

"You boosted it?" I said.

"'Course. Ain't gonna fuck up my own wheels, man."

"'Course not," I said. "I wonder if they've fished that guy out of the Charles yet."

Hawk grinned. "Damn," he said. "Wish the fuzz had been a little slower. I was gonna throw 'em all in."

CHAPTER 13

We wandered in a mazy motion through the MIT complex down to Kendall Square and caught the subway to Park Street. We walked up across the Common to Beacon, where Hawk's car was parked in front of the State House by a sign that said RESERVED FOR MEMBERS OF THE GENERAL COURT. It was a silver-gray Jaguar XJ 12.

Hawk said, "You owe me two bills, babe."

I said, "Gimme a ride to Susan's house."

"Smithfield?"

"Yeah."

"That's the woods, man. That's your fucking forest primeval out there."

"Hawk, it's thirteen miles north. We could run it in about two hours."

"Dinner," Hawk said. "Dinner and some champagne, I buy the champagne. They sell champagne out in the woods, babe?"

"We can stop at the trading post," I said. "Cost plenty wampum, though."

We got in and Hawk put the Jag in gear and we purred north over the Mystic Bridge. Hawk put an Olatunji tape on and the car trembled with percussion all the way to Saugus, where Hawk pulled into a Martignetti's off Route 1 and bought three bottles of

Taittinger Blanc de Blancs. At forty-five bucks a bottle it was cutting a lot of profit off the two hundred I was paying him. He also brought out two six-packs of Beck's beer.

"No point wasting the champagne on you," he said. "You born beer, you gonna die beer. There's a bottle opener in the glove compartment."

Hawk peeled the foil off the neck of one bottle of Taittinger and twisted the cork out with a pop. I opened a bottle of beer. Hawk drank from the neck of his forty-five-dollar champagne bottle as he tooled the Jaguar up Route 1. I drank some Beck's.

"Difference between you and me, babe," Hawk said, "right here." He drank some more champagne.

"As long as there is one," I said. "Any difference will do."

Hawk laughed quietly and turned his Olatunji tape up louder. It was a quarter to six when we pulled into Susan's driveway. My MG was there beside the car Susan had bought to replace the MG. It was a big red Ford Bronco with a white roof and four-wheel drive and heavy-duty this and that, and big tires with raised white letters.

Hawk looked at it and said, "What the fuck is that?"

I said, "That's Suze's new vehicle. For Christmas I'm getting her some foxtails and a pair of big rubber dice."

"That's a big ten-four momma," Hawk said.

We went in. Susan was the only person I've ever seen that Hawk seemed to have any feeling about. He grinned when he saw her. She said, "Hawk," and came over and kissed him. He gave her the two unopened bottles of champagne.

"Brought us a present," he said. "Spenser promised supper."

She looked at me. "What am I, Howard Johnson's," she said.

"You're a real looker when you're angry," I said.

She took the champagne and went toward the kitchen, "Goddamn host of the goddamn highway," she said.

"You forgot to take my beer," I said.

She kept going. Hawk and I went into the living room. Paul was watching a bowling show on television. Patty was sipping what looked like bourbon on the rocks.

"This is Hawk," I said. "Patty Giacomin and her son, Paul."

Paul looked at Hawk and then looked back at the bowling show. Patty smiled and started to get up and changed her mind and stayed seated.

"Are you the other one?" she said.

Hawk said, "Yes." He drank some champagne from the bottle.

Susan came back into the room with another bottle of champagne in a bucket and four fluted champagne glasses on a tole serving tray.

"Perhaps you'd care to try a glass," she said to Hawk.

" 'Spect ah might, Missy Susan," Hawk said.

Susan said to Patty, "May Paul have a glass?"

Patty said, "Oh, sure."

Susan said, "Would you care for a glass, Paul?"

Paul said, "Okay."

Patty Giacomin said to Hawk, "I'd like to thank you for what you did today."

Hawk said, "You're welcome."

"I really mean it," Patty said. "It was so brave, I was so terrified. You were wonderful to help."

"Spenser gave me two hundred dollars," Hawk said. "I figure it'll show up in his expense voucher."

"Are you a detective too?" Patty said.

Hawk smiled. "No," he said. "No, I am not." His face was bright with mirth.

I said, "I'm going to put this beer away," and went into the kitchen. Susan came out behind me.

"Just what in hell do you think we're going to feed these people?" Susan said.

"Got any cake?" I said.

"I'm serious. I don't have anything in the house to serve five people."

"I'll go get something," I said.

"And let me entertain your guests?"

"Your choice," I said. "I don't care to have a fight though."

"Well, don't do this to me. I don't simply sit around here waiting for your problems to drop by."

"Love me, love my problems," I said.

"Sometimes I wonder if that's a worthwhile trade-off."

"There you go," I said, "talking that education management jargon again."

She was looking in the refrigerator. "If I want to say trade-off, goddammit, I'll say trade-off. I've got some of that Williamsburg bacon. We could make up a bunch of BLTs."

"Toasted," I said. "And on the side, some of those homemade bread-and-butter pickles we did last fall."

"And cut flowers in a vase, and the Meyer Davis Orchestra? You better go back in and help out on the conversation. Hawk must be ready to jump out of his skin."

"Not Hawk," I said. "He doesn't mind silence. He doesn't want to talk. He won't talk. He doesn't sweat small talk much."

"He doesn't sweat anything too much," Susan said, "does he?"

"Nope. He's completely inside. Come on in and talk a bit, then we'll all transfer to the kitchen and make sandwiches and eat. There's some cheese too, and a couple of apples. It'll be a feast." I patted her lightly on the backside. "Besides, we need your advice."

"My advice to you, big fella, is to keep your hands to yourself," she said.

I opened another beer and we went back into the living room. Hawk was stretched out in a wing chair near the fireplace, feet straight out in front of him, body slumped easily in the chair. When we came in, he took a small sip from his champagne glass and put it back on the end table near him. Patty and Paul were watching the six o'clock news. No one was talking.

I sat in a Boston rocker on the opposite side of the fireplace from Hawk.

I said, "Paul, you did good today."

He nodded.

"Patty," I said, "tell me what happened."

"I came out of the supermarket and three men with guns made me get into the car. That one that came to our house was one of them."

"Buddy?" I said.

"Yes. He sat in front with the driver and the other man sat in back with me and we drove to a pay phone in Boston. Then we drove to the bridge and they told me to get out and start walking. Other than that they didn't talk to me at all or say anything."

"You recognize any of them, Hawk?"

"Dude I threw in the river is Richie Vega. He used to shake down massage parlors."

Patty said, "My God, how would Mel find people like that to hire?"

Hawk raised his head slightly and looked at me. I shrugged. Hawk let his chin settle back onto his chest.

Patty Giacomin said to Hawk, "Do you know my husband?"

Hawk said, "No. Not if he go by Mel Giacomin."

"Well, that's his name."

Hawk nodded.

Patty said, "Do you know what this is all about?"

Hawk said, "No."

"You got in a fight with three men and they had guns, and you threw one into the river, and you don't even know why?"

Hawk said, "Yeah, that's right."

"And you're not a detective or anything?"

"Nope."

Paul was watching and listening. We had distracted him from the tube.

"A strong-arm man?" he said.

"Yeah, something like that," I said.

The newscasters joked painfully with the weather forecaster on television.

I said to Susan, "I don't know how much Patty's told you since she arrived, but for your benefit and Hawk's I'll run through it very quickly."

I did.

When I got through, there was silence. Hawk seemed almost asleep. Only the evening news mewled in one corner.

Susan said, "You can't continue this way. You and your husband will have to negotiate."

"After what he pulled today?" Patty said. "I will not talk to that man."

"What about the law?" Susan said.

"The law has already given me custody."

"But kidnapping," Susan said. "Kidnapping is illegal."

"You mean report him to the police."

"Certainly. You can identify at least two of the men. Hawk and Spenser can testify that they had indeed kidnapped you. Surely the police could trace it back to your husband."

Susan looked at me. I nodded. Hawk sipped champagne and put the glass back gently on the end table. He was nearly prone in the chair, his feet stretched out and crossed at the ankles.

"He'd kill me," Patty said.

"You mean you're afraid to tell the police because of what your husband would do?"

"Yes. He'd be furious. He'd . . . I can't do that."

"But he's already had you kidnapped. Aren't you already afraid of him?"

"But he wouldn't try to hurt me. If I told, he'd . . . I can't. I can't do that."

"So do you plan to employ me permanently?" I said.

"I can't. I can't keep paying you. I'm . . . running out of money."

Hawk smiled to himself. I looked at Susan.

She said, "What about Paul? How can he grow up like this?"

Patty Giacomin shook her head.

We were all quiet. Paul was watching the television again. The network news was on now. Authoritative.

Patty said, "It isn't me he wants. It's Paul. If I told on him . . ."

"The heat would be on you," I said. "Instead of on Paul."

Susan said, "That's it, isn't it?"

Patty shook her head. "I don't know," she said. "What difference does it make? I'm not going to the police. I'm not." Her voice was shaky. "I've still got money. We'll do something."

I said, "What?"

She said, "You take Paul."

"Take him where?" I said.

"I don't know. Anywhere. I'll pay you," she said.

"I hide Paul out so your husband can't find him?"

"Yes. I'll pay you."

"Why won't they just try the same swap again that they tried today?"

"I'll go live with a friend. Mel won't find me."

"So why not take Paul too," I said. "Much cheaper."

"He won't let me bring Paul."

"Your friend?"

"Yes."

"That wouldn't be old disco Stephen, would it? The one I met when I first brought Paul home?"

She nodded.

I said, "Probably afraid if it got too crowded, his cashmere sweaters would wrinkle."

"He's not like that. You don't know him," she said.

"Well, a friend in need . . ." I said.

"Will you take Paul?" Patty said.

I looked at him. He was staring hard at the network news. His shoulders were stiff and awkward. He was concentrating on ignoring us.

"Sure," I said. "It would be a pleasure."

Susan looked at me with her eyes widened. Hawk

made a sound under his breath like a soft hog call.

"He ain't heavy," I said at large. "He's my brother."

Susan shook her head.

CHAPTER 14

We ate our BLTs and drank champagne in the kitchen without much talk.

For an extra fifty dollars Hawk said he'd take Paul and his mother home and stay there till I arrived. Neither of the Giacomins looked very happy with that, but they went.

"Don't be scared," Hawk said as they left. "Some of my best friends are honkies."

Patty Giacomin looked at me.

"It's okay," I said. "He's nearly as good as I am. In the dark maybe better. You'll be fine."

Paul looked at me. "When am I going to stay with you?" he said.

"Tomorrow. I'll be home later tonight and tomorrow we'll pack up and go."

"He be around, kid," Hawk said. "One thing about old Spenser, he predictable. He say he going to do something. He do it." Hawk shook his head. "Dumb," he said.

They went out. Susan and I stood in the doorway and watched them. Susan waved. Then Hawk's Jag murmured into gear and they were gone. I closed the door and turned and picked Susan up in my arms.

"Couch or bed, little lady," I said.

"God, you're masterful," she said.

"Maybe you could kick your little feet and pound prettily on my chest with your little fists?" I said.

"Be happy I don't apply heel to groin," she said, "after all the goddamned unannounced company."

"You mean I'm going to have to force my attentions upon you?" I said.

"Yes," she said. "But you may as well force them in the bedroom. It's more comfortable."

I walked toward the hall with her. "You smell good," I said.

"I know," she said. "Halston."

The bedroom door was ajar. I pushed it open with my foot and walked in.

"You better kiss me," she said. "Stifle my screams."

I sat on the edge of the bed and kissed her. I kept my eyes open. In the light from the hall I could see that she closed hers. She moved her head away and opened her eyes and looked up at my face.

I said, "Lipwise you've still got it, baby."

Her face was serious and still, but her eyes glittered. "You ain't seen nothing yet," she said.

It was late when we were through. Most of our clothing was scattered about and the bedspread was badly wrinkled. I lay on my back with my heart pounding and my chest heaving in air. Susan lay beside me. She held my hand.

"Have you overexerted?" she said.

"Your resistance was fierce," I said.

"Umm," she said.

From the living room there was the faint sound of the television, which Paul had left on. The image of it gesticulating to an empty room pleased me.

"Just what do you plan to do with that boy, cookie?" Susan said.

"I thought we might want to talk that out," I said.

"We?"

"You know about kids."

"I know about guidance," Susan said. "There's a difference."

"I'll need help."

"You'll need more than that. The boy is bound to be difficult. Even without knowing him one could predict that. My God, he's chattel in a divorce settlement. What do you know about the needs of a neurotic adolescent?"

"I thought I'd ask you," I said.

"Based on my experience with you?" she said.

"I'm not neurotic," I said.

Susan turned her face toward me. In the half-light she was smiling. She squeezed my hand. "No," she said, "you aren't. You're complicated, but you are not even a little bit neurotic."

"The kid needs to get away from his parents," I said.

"That's not the conventional wisdom, except in cases more extreme than this."

"Maybe the conventional wisdom is right," I said, "if the choice is to get into the welfare-youth services—foster-home system."

"But not if he's going to be with you?"

"Not if he's going to be with me," I said.

"You think you can make life better for him?"

"Yes."

"How long do you plan to keep him?"

"I don't know."

"It's hard enough to raise children you love," Susan said. "I've seen it from the failure end, over and over, parents whose kids are just a goddamned mess. Parents who love them and have presided over the complete botching of their lives. I think your eyes are bigger than your stomach on this one, dear heart."

"How about that property in Maine," I said.

Susan propped up on one elbow. "Fryeburg?" she said.

"Yeah. I told you I'd build a house on it."

"When you got a chance, you said."

"This is the chance."

"You and Paul?"

"Yes."

She was quiet, lying naked beside me, on her right side with her head propped on her right elbow. Her lipstick was smeared. The intelligence in her face was like energy. It seemed almost to shimmer. That she was beautiful was only the first thing you noticed.

"Work release," she said.

"The kid's never been taught how to act," I said. "He doesn't know anything. He's got no pride. He's got nothing he's good at. He's got nothing but the tube."

"And you plan to teach him."

"I'll teach him what I know. I know how to do carpentry. I know how to cook. I know how to punch. I know how to act."

"You're not so bad in the rack either, big fella."

I grinned. "We'll let him work that out on his own, maybe."

She shook her head. "You make it sound simple. It's not. You don't teach people unless they want to learn. It's not just an intellectual exercise. It's a matter of emotion, of psychology. I mean the boy may be positively pathological."

"He's got nothing to lose," I said. "Compared to an afternoon of game shows on TV, anything is up. For crissake, the kid watches soap operas," I said.

"So do I," Susan said.

"Well, your degeneracy is already established," I said. "Besides you do others things."

"Only with you, sweet potato."

"You want to get in on this?" I said.

"The salvation of Paul Giacomin?"

"Yeah."

"I'm willing to consult," she said. "But I don't want to see you overinvested in this. The chances of success are slight. What happens if next week his mother runs out of money?"

"We'll worry about that when it happens."

"It'll happen soon," Susan said.

"Woman's intuition?"

"Believe me," Susan said. "It'll be soon."

I shrugged.

"You'll keep him anyway," she said.

I didn't say anything.

"You will," she said, "you big goddamned sap. You know you will."

"He needs to grow up quick," I said. "He needs to get autonomous. It's the only hope he's got. For him he's gotta stop being a kid at fifteen. His parents are shit. He can't depend on them anymore, He's gotta get autonomous."

"And you're going to show him how?"

"Yes."

"Well, no one better. You're the most autonomous human being I've ever seen. It's a grim prospect for a fifteen-year-old boy though."

"How do you like his prospects if he doesn't grow up quick?"

Susan was quiet, looking down at me. "Spring will be a little late this year," she said.

"For Paul? Yeah." I laughed with no pleasure. "Spring is gone. It's early autumn for Paul. If I can do it."

"And if he can," Susan said.

CHAPTER 15

It was early May and the sun was thick and warm. The forsythias had begun. The birds were about and the joggers were out of their sweat pants, legs gleaming white in the spring sun. Paul Giacomin came out of his house with a big green plaid suitcase and a white drawstring laundry bag. He was still wearing his pea coat. He needed a haircut. His corduroy pants were too short. He was straining to carry the two bags.

I was driving Susan's Bronco. I got out and took the suitcase from Paul and put it in the back. He stuck the laundry bag in beside it and left the drawstring hanging out over the tailgate. I flipped the string inside and put the power window up with the key. Patty Giacomin came out and stood by the Bronco. Pale green slacks, lavender shirt, white blazer. Big sunglasses, bright lipstick. Stephen was with her. He was as beautiful as she—jeans with a Pierre Cardin patch on them, Frye boots, a half-buttoned tailored collarless shirt in vertical blue-on-blue stripes, a gray sharkskin vest, unbuttoned. His dark maroon Pontiac Firebird was parked in the Giacomin driveway.

"The Firebird's not right," I said. "It doesn't go with the rest of the look."

"Oh, really," Stephen said. "What would you suggest?"

"A Z maybe, or a Porsche. Extend that clean sophisticated continental look, you know?"

Stephen smiled. "Perhaps," he said.

Patty said to her son, "I'll write you a letter.".

He nodded. She made an awkward gesture of hugging him. But she didn't seem able to carry through and ended up putting one arm across his shoulders for a moment and patting him slightly on the back. He stood silently while this happened. Then he got into the Bronco. The high step into the front seat was difficult and he had to struggle, and finally squirm up onto the seat. I got in the driver's side.

Patty said, "Bye."

Paul said, "Bye," and we drove off. As we turned off Emerson Road I saw tears fill Paul's eyes. I kept watching the road. He didn't cry. We took Route 3 to 495, 495 to 95 and went north on 95 to the Portsmouth Circle. In that time Paul didn't say anything. He sat and stared out the window at the unvarying landscaping along the highways. I plugged a Johnny Hartman tape into the stereo on the assumption that it was never too soon to start his education. He paid no attention. At the Portsmouth Circle we took the Spaulding Turnpike and then Route 16. We were in rural New England now. An hour from Boston cows grazed. There were barns and feed stores and towns with a mill that no longer milled at the center.

We got to North Conway, New Hampshire, about one thirty in the afternoon. I stopped at a restaurant called Horsefeathers opposite the green in the center of town. There was a softball diamond on the green and some kids were playing a game without umpires.

I said, "Let's eat."

He said nothing, but got out of the car and went into the restaurant with me. We'd been in rural New England. Now we were in rural chic. North Conway is a major ski resort in the winter, and summer homes abound around it in New Hampshire and across the border in Maine. Horsefeathers had brass and hanging plants and looked just like restaurants in San Francisco.

The food was good and at two twenty we were in the car again heading for Fryeburg. At a quarter to three we were parked at the edge of Kimball Lake. The land Susan had gotten from her husband as part of the divorce settlement was nearly three quarters of an acre at the end of a dirt road with woods all around. There were cabins along the lake close enough to keep you from feeling like Henry Thoreau, but it was secluded. Susan's ex-husband had used the place for hunting and fishing. At one edge of the property he'd built a small cabin with running lake water for showering, a well for drinking water, electricity, and a flush toilet, but no central heat. There was a free-standing fireplace in the living room, a small electric stove and an old electric refrigerator in the galleylike kitchen, and two small bedrooms with metal bunk beds in them, and no closets. Susan and I came up occasionally to cook steaks over a wood fire, swim in the lake, and stroll in the woods until the bugs closed in.

Paul said, "We're gonna stay here?"

"Yes. We'll live in that cabin and tomorrow we'll start building a new and better one."

Paul said, "What do you mean?"

I said, "We're going to build a house. You and me."

"We can't do that."

"Yeah, we can. I know how. I'll teach you."

"How do you know how to build a house?"

"My father was a carpenter."

The kid just looked at me. It never occurred to him that houses were built by people. Sometimes they were built by construction companies and sometimes they probably just generated spontaneously.

"Come on, unload. We're going to be very busy up here. There's a lot to do."

"I don't want to build a house," Paul said.

"I'll need help. I can't do it alone. It'll be good to work with your hands. You'll like it."

"I won't."

I shrugged. "We'll see," I said. "Help me unload."

The back seat of the Bronco folded forward, leaving a lot of cargo space. The cargo space was full. There was the big old tool chest that had been my father's. And there was a radial arm saw I'd bought last year and used in Susan's cellar sometimes. There was also a set of barbells, a weight bench, a heavy bag, a speed bag, my suitcase, a large green cooler with perishables in it, a big carton with other food, a pump-action Ithaca shotgun, ammunition, some fishing equipment, two sleeping bags, some boots, a five-cell flashlight, an ax, some books, a machete, a carton of records, two shovels, a mattock, and one hundred feet of rope.

I unlocked the cabin and opened all the windows. We started to carry and stow. A lot of the things were too heavy for Paul and everything he carried he seemed to handle badly. He picked things up only with the tips of his fingers. When I told him to take the shotgun in, he carried it awkwardly by the butt rather than where it balanced. He carried one of the shovels by its blade. When we were through, there was sweat on his face and he seemed red and hot. He still wore his pea coat.

It was after five when we finished. The bugs were out and it was getting cool. Last fall Susan and I had bought a cheap stereo and put it in the cabin. I put on the Benny Goodman 1938 jazz concert while I made a fire. I had a beer while I started supper. Paul came in from looking at the lake and got a Coke out of the refrigerator. He went into the living room. In a minute he was back.

"Didn't you bring a television?" he said.

"No," I said.

He snorted angrily and went back in the living room. I figured he'd stare at the record player. Anything in a pinch.

I opened a large can of beans and put them in a pan to heat. While they heated I put out some pickles and rye bread, ketchup, plates, and utensils. Then I panfried two steaks. We ate at a table in the living room, the kitchen was too small, listening to the Goodman band, watching the fire move, and smelling the wood smoke. Paul still wore the pea coat although the room was warm from the fire.

After supper I got out my book and started to read. Paul picked up the record albums and looked at them and put them back in disgust. He looked out the window. He went outside to look around but came back in almost at once. The bugs were out as it got dark.

"You shoulda brought a TV," he said once.

"Read," I said. "There's books there."

"I don't like to read."

"It's better than looking at the lamp fixtures till bedtime, isn't it?"

"No."

I kept reading.

Paul said, "What's that book?"

"*A Distant Mirror*," I said.

"What's it about?"

"The fourteenth century."

He was quiet. Sap oozed out of the end of a log and sputtered onto the hot ash beneath it.

"What do you want to read about the fourteen hundreds for?" Paul said.

"Thirteen hundreds," I said. "Just like the nineteen hundreds are the twentieth century."

Paul shrugged. "So why do you want to read about it?"

I put the book down. "I like to know what life was like for them," I said. "I like the sense of connection over six hundred years that I can get."

"I think it's boring," Paul said.

"Compared to what?" I said.

He shrugged.

"I think it's boring compared to taking Susan Silverman to Paris," I said. "Things are relative."

He didn't say anything.

"I know more about being human when I know more about their lives. I get a certain amount of perspective. The time was full of people that killed, tortured, suffered, struggled, and agonized for things that seemed worth anything to them. Now they've been dead for six hundred years. What's it all about, Ozymandias?"

"Huh?"

" 'Ozymandias'? It's a poem. Here, I'll show you." I

got up and found a book in the box I hadn't un-
packed yet.

"Listen," I said. I read the poem to him. Deliberately in the firelit room. It was about his level.

He said, "She your girl friend?"

I said, "What?"

He said, "Susan Silverman. She your girl friend?"

"Yes," I said.

"You going to get married?"

"I don't know."

"You love her?"

"Yes."

"How about her?" he said.

"Does she love me?"

He nodded.

"Yes," I said.

"Then why don't you get married?"

"I'm not sure. Mostly it's a question of how we'd af-
fect each other, I suppose. Would I interfere with her
work? Would she interfere with mine? That sort of
thing."

"Wouldn't she quit work?"

"No."

"Why not? I would. I wouldn't work if I didn't
have to."

"She likes her work. Makes her feel good about
herself. Me too. If you just did it for money, of course
you'd want to quit. But if you do it because you like
to . . ." I gestured with my hand. "What do you
like to do?"

He shrugged. "That guy Hawk your friend?"

"Sort of."

"You like him?"

"Sort of. I can count on him."

"He seems scary to me."

"Well, he is. He's not good. But he's a good man. You know the difference?"

"No."

"You will," I said. "It's a difference I'm going to help you learn."

CHAPTER 16

The next morning I woke Paul up at seven.

"Why do I have to get up?" he said. "There's no school."

"We got a lot to do," I said.

"I don't want to get up."

"Well, you have to. I'm going to make breakfast. Anything special you want?"

"I don't want any."

"Okay," I said. "But there's nothing to eat till lunch."

He stared at me, squinting, and not entirely awake.

I went out to the kitchen and mixed up some batter for corn bread. While the bread was baking and the coffee perking, I took a shower and dressed, took the corn bread out, and went into Paul's room. He had gone back to sleep. I shook him awake.

"Come on, kid," I said. "I know you don't want to, but you have to. You'll get used to the schedule. Eventually you'll even like it."

Paul pushed his head deeper into the sleeping bag and shook his head.

"Yeah," I said. "You gotta. Once you're up and showered you'll feel fine. Don't make me get tough."

"What'll you do if I don't," Paul muttered into the sleeping bag.

"Pull you out," I said. "Hold you under the shower. Dry you, dress you, Et cetera."

"I won't get up," he said.

I pulled him out, undressed him, and held him under the shower, It took about a half an hour. It's not easy to control someone, even a kid, if you don't want to hurt them. I shampooed his hair and held him under to rinse, then I pulled him out and handed him a towel.

"You want me to dress you?" I said.

He shook his head, and wrapped the towel around himself, and went to his room. I went to the kitchen and put out the corn bread and strawberry jam and a bowl of assorted fruit. While I waited for him I ate an orange and a banana. I poured a cup of coffee. I sipped a little of it. I had not warned him against going back to bed. Somehow I'd had a sense that would be insulting. I wanted him to come out on his own. If he didn't I had lost some ground. I sipped some more coffee. The corn bread was cooling. I looked at his bedroom door. I didn't like cool corn bread.

The bedroom door opened and he came out. He had on jeans that had obviously been shortened and then let down again, his worn Top-Siders, and a green polo shirt with a penguin on the left breast.

"You want coffee or milk?" I said.

"Coffee."

I poured some. "What do you take in it?" I said.

"I don't know," he said. "I never had it before."

"May as well start with cream and sugar," I said. "Calories aren't your problem."

"You think I'm skinny?"

"Yes. There's corn bread, jam, fruit, and coffee. Help yourself."

"I don't want anything."

I said, "Okay," and started on the corn bread. Paul sipped at the coffee. He didn't look like he liked it. After breakfast I cleaned up the dishes and said to Paul, "You got any sneakers?"

"No."

"Okay, first thing we'll do is go over to North Conway and buy you some."

"I don't need any," he said.

"Yes, you do," I said. "We'll pick up a newspaper too."

"How you know they sell them over there?"

"North Conway? They probably got more flashy running shoes than aspirin," I said. "We'll find some."

On the ride to North Conway Paul said, "How come you made me get up like that?"

"Two reasons," I said. "One, you need some structure in your life, some scheduling, to give you a sense of order. Two, I was going to have to do it sometime. I figured I might as well get it over with."

"You wouldn't have to do it if you let me sleep."

"It would've been something. You'd push me until you found out how far I'd go. You have to test me, so you can trust me."

"What are you, a child psychologist?"

"No. Susan told me that."

"Well, she's crazy."

"I know you don't know any better, but that's against the rules."

"What?"

"Speaking badly of another person's beloved, you know? I don't want you to speak ill of her." We were in Fryeburg Center.

"Sorry."

"Okay."

We were quiet as we drove through the small open town with its pleasant buildings. It was maybe fifteen minutes to North Conway. We bought Paul a pair of Nike LDVs just like mine except size 7, and a pair of sweat pants.

"You got a jock?" I said.

Paul looked embarrassed. He shook his head. We bought one of them and two pairs of white sweat socks. I paid and we drove back to Fryeburg. It was ten when we got to the cabin. I handed him his bag of stuff.

"Go put this stuff on and we'll have a run," I said.

"A run?"

"Yeah."

"I can't run," he said.

"You can learn," I said.

"I don't want to."

"I know, but we'll take it easy. We won't go far. We'll run a little, walk a little. Do a little more each day. You'll feel good."

"You going to make me?" Paul said.

"Yes."

He went very slowly into the cabin. I went in with him. He went into his room. I went into mine. In about twenty minutes he came out with the new jogging shoes looking ridiculously yellow and the new sweat pants slightly too big for his thin legs, and his scrawny upper body pale and shivery-looking in the spring sun. I was dressed the same, but my stuff wasn't new.

"We'll stretch," I said. "Bend your knees until you can touch the ground with both hands easily. Like this. Good. Now without taking your hands from the ground, try to straighten your knees. Don't strain, just steady pressure. We'll hold it thirty seconds."

"What's that for?" he said.

"Loosen up the lower back and the hamstring muscles in the back of your thighs. Now squat, like this, let your butt hang down toward the ground and hold that for thirty seconds. It does somewhat the same thing."

I showed him how to stretch the calf muscles and loosen up the quadriceps. He did everything very awkwardly and tentatively as if he wanted to prove he couldn't. I didn't comment on that. I was figuring out how to run with a gun. I normally didn't. But I wasn't normally looking after anyone but me when I ran.

"Okay," I said. "We're ready for a short slow run. Wait till I get something in the house." I went in and got my gun. It was a short Smith & Wesson .38. I took it from its holster, checked the load, and went out carrying it in my hand.

"You going to run with that?" Paul said.

"Best I could think of," I said. "I'll just carry it in my hand." I held it by the cylinder and trigger guard, not by the handle. It was not conspicuous.

"You afraid they'll find us?"

"No, but no harm to be safe. When you can, it's better to deal with possibilities than likelihoods."

"Huh?"

"Come on, we'll jog. I'll explain while we run."

We started at a slow pace. Paul looked as if he might never have run before. His movements seemed unsynchronized, and he took each step as if he had to think about it first.

"Say when you need to walk," I said. "There's no hurry."

He nodded.

I said, "When you're thinking about something important, like if your father might try to kidnap you again, it's better to think of what the best thing would be to do if he tried, rather than trying to decide how likely he was to try. You can't decide if he'll try, that's up to him. You decide what to do if he does. That's up to you. Understand?"

He nodded. Already I could see he was too winded to talk.

"A way of living better is to make the decisions you need to make based on what you can control. When you can."

We were jogging up a dirt road that led from the cabin to a larger dirt road. It was maybe half a mile long. On either side there were dogberry bushes and small birch and maple saplings under the tall white pines and maples that hovered above us. There were raspberry bushes too, just starting to bud. It was cool under the dappling of the trees, but not cold.

"We'll hang a right here," I said, "and head along this road a ways. No need to push. Stop when you feel the need and we'll walk a ways." He nodded again. The road was larger now. It circled the lake, side roads spoking off to cabins every hundred yards. The names of the cabin owners were painted on hokey rustic signs and nailed to a tree at the head of each side road. We had gone maybe a mile when Paul stopped running. He bent over holding his side.

"Stitch?"

He nodded.

"Don't bend forward," I said. "Bend backward. As far back as you can. It'll stretch it out."

He did what I told him. I hadn't thought he would. An old logging road ran up to our left. We turned up it. Paul walking with his back arched.

"How far did we run?"

"About a mile," I said. "Damn good for the first time out."

"How far can you run?"

"Ten, fifteen miles, I don't know for sure."

Walking on a felled log, we crossed a small ravine where the spring melt was still surging down toward the lake. In a month it would be dry and dusty in there.

"Let's head back," I said. "Maybe when we get back to the road you can run a little more."

Paul didn't say anything. A redheaded woodpecker rattled against a tree beside us. When we got back to the road I moved into a slow jog again. Paul walked a few more feet and then he cranked into a jerky slow run behind me. We went maybe half a mile to the side road leading to our cabin. I stopped the jog and began to walk. Paul stopped running the moment I did.

When we were back to the cabin, I said, "Put on a sweat shirt or a light jacket or something. Then we'll set up some equipment."

I put on a blue sweat shirt with the sleeves cut off. Paul put on a gray long-sleeved sweat shirt with a New England Patriots emblem on the front. The sleeves were too long.

We brought out the weight bench, the heavy bag, the speed bag and its strike board, and the tool chest. Paul carried one end of the tool chest and one end of the weight bench.

"We'll hang the heavy bag off this tree branch," I said. "And we'll fasten the speed bag to the trunk."

Paul nodded.

"And we'll put the weight bench here under the tree out of the way of the heavy bag. If it rains we'll toss a tarp over it."

Paul nodded.

"And when we get it set up, I'll show you how to use it."

Paul nodded again. I didn't know if I was making progress or not. I seemed to have broken his spirit.

"How's that sound, kid?" I said.

He shrugged. Maybe I hadn't broken his spirit.

CHAPTER 17

It took about an hour to set up. Most of that time was spent getting the speed bag mounted. I finally nailed through the strike board into two thick branches that veered out at about the right height. For me. For Paul we'd have to get a box to stand on. It took three trips in and out for me to get the weights out. Paul carried some of the small dumbbells. I carried the bar with as many plates as I could on either end, and then went back and carried out the rest of the plates in a couple of trips.

"Now, after lunch," I said, "we'll work out for a couple of hours and then knock off for the day. Normally we'd do this in the morning and build the house in the afternoon, but we got a late start today because we had to get you outfitted, so we'll start the house tomorrow afternoon."

For lunch we had feta cheese and Syrian bread with pickles, olives, cherry tomatoes, and cucumber wedges. Paul had milk. I had beer. Paul said the cheese smelled bad. There were a couple of camp chairs outside the cabin, and after lunch we went out and sat in them. It was one thirty. I turned on the portable radio. The Sox were playing the Tigers.

Paul said, "I don't like baseball."

"Don't listen."

"But I can't help it if it's on."

"Okay, a bargain. I like the ball game. You like what?"

"I don't care."

"Okay. I'll listen to the ball game when it's on. You can listen to whatever you want to any other time. Fair?"

Paul shrugged. On the lake a loon made its funny sound.

"That's a loon," I said. Paul nodded.

"I don't want to lift weights," Paul said. "I don't want to learn to hit the punching bags. I don't like that stuff."

"What would you rather do?" I said.

"I don't know."

"We'll only do it on weekdays. We'll take Saturday and Sunday off and do other stuff."

"What?"

"Anything you want. We'll go look at things. We'll fish, shoot, go to museums, swim when the weather's warmer, see a ball game in case you learn to like them, eat out, see a movie, go to a play, go down to Boston and hang around. Have I hit anything you like yet?"

Paul shrugged. I nodded. By two thirty the Sox were three runs ahead behind Eckersley and our lunch had settled.

"Let's get to it," I said. "We'll do three sets of each exercise to start with. We'll do bench presses, curls, pullovers, flyes, some shrugs, some sit-ups. We'll work out combinations on the heavy bag and I'll show you how to work the speed bag."

I hung a big canteen of water on one of the tree branches. It was covered with red-striped blanket material and it always made me feel like Kit Carson to drink from it.

"Drink all the water you want. Rest in between times. No hurry. We got the rest of the day."

"I don't know how to do any of those things."

"I know. I'll show you. First we'll see how much you can work with. We'll start with bench presses."

I put the big York bar on the bench rests with no weight on it.

"Try that," I said.

"Without any weights?"

"It's heavy enough. Try it for starters. If it's too light we can add poundage."

"What do I do?"

"I'll show you." I lay on my back on the bench, took the barbell in a medium-wide grip, lifted it off the rack, lowered it to my chest, and pushed it straight up to arms' length. Then I lowered it to my chest and pushed it up again. "Like so," I said. "Try to do it ten times if you can."

I put the bar back on the rack and got up. Paul lay on the bench.

"Where do I hold it?"

"Spread your hands a little, like that. That's good. Keep your thumbs in, like this, so if it's too heavy it won't break your thumbs. I'll spot you here."

"What's spot?"

"I'll have a hand on it to be sure you don't drop it on yourself."

Paul wrestled it off the rack. It was too heavy for him. His thin arms shook with the strain as he lowered it to his narrow chest. I had a hand lightly at the midpoint of the bar.

"Okay," I said. "Good. Good. Now push it up.

Breathe in, now blow out and shove the bar up, shove, blow, shove." I did some cheerleading.

Paul arched his back and struggled. His arms shook more. I put a little pressure under the bar and helped him. He got it extended.

"Now onto the rack," I said. I helped him guide it over and set it in its place. His face was very red.

"Good," I said. "Next time we'll do two."

"I can't even do it," he said.

"Sure you can. You just did it."

"You helped me."

"Just a bit. One of the things about weights is you make progress fast at first. It's encouraging."

"I can't even lift it without the weights," he said.

"In a couple of months you'll be pressing more than your own weight," I said. "Come on. We'll do another one."

He tried again. This time I had to help him more.

"I'm getting worse," he said.

"Naturally, you're getting tired. The third try will be even harder. That's the point. You work the muscle when it's tired and it breaks down faster and new muscle builds up quicker." I was beginning to sound like Arnold Schwarzenegger. Paul lay red-faced and silent on the bench. There were fine blue veins under the near-translucent skin of his chest. The collarbone, the ribs, and the sternum were all clearly defined against the tight skin. He didn't weigh a hundred pounds.

"Last try," I said. He took the bar off its rest and this time I had to keep it from dropping on him. "Up now," I said, "blow it up. This is the one that counts most. Come on, come on, up, up, up. Good. Good."

We set the bar back on the bench. Paul sat up. His arms were still trembling slightly.

"You do some," he said.

I nodded. I put two fifty-pound plates on each end of the bar and lay on the bench. I lifted the weight off the cradle and brought it to my chest.

"Watch which muscles move," I said to Paul, "that way you learn which exercise does what for you." I pressed the bar up, let it down, pressed it up. I breathed out each time. I did ten repetitions and set the bar back on the rack. A faint sweat had started on my forehead. Above us in the maple tree a grosbeak with a rose-colored breast fluttered in and sat. I did another set. The sweat began to film on my chest. The mild breeze cooled it.

Paul said, "How much can you lift?"

I said, "I don't know exactly. It's sort of a good idea not to worry about that. You do better to exercise with what you can handle and not be looking to see who can lift more and who can't and how much you can lift. I can lift more than this."

"How much is that?"

"Two hundred forty-five pounds."

"Does Hawk lift weights?"

"Some."

"Can he lift as much as you?"

"Probably."

I did a third set. When I got through I was puffing a little, and the sweat was trickling down my chest.

"Now we do some curls," I said. I showed him how. We couldn't find a dumbbell light enough for him to curl with one hand, so he used both hands on one dumbbell.

After two hours Paul sat on the weight bench with his head hanging, forearms on his thighs, puffing as if he'd run a long way. I sat beside him. We had finished the weights. I handed Paul the canteen. He drank a little and handed it back to me. I drank and hung it back up.

"How you feel?" I said.

Paul just shook his head without looking up.

"That good, huh? Well, you'll be stiff tomorrow. Come on. We'll play with the bags a little."

"I don't want to do any more."

"I know, but another half hour and you'll have done it all. This will be fun. We won't have to work hard."

"Why don't you just let me alone?"

I sat back down beside him. "Because everybody has left you alone all your life and you are, now, as a result, in a mess. I'm going to get you out of it."

"Whaddya mean?"

"I mean you don't have anything to care about. You don't have anything to be proud of. You don't have anything to know. You are almost completely neutral because nobody took the time to teach you or show you and because what you saw of the people who brought you up didn't offer anything you wanted to copy."

"It's not my fault."

"No, not yet. But if you lay back and let oblivion roll over you, it will be your fault. You're old enough now to start becoming a person. And you're old enough now so that you'll have to start taking some kind of responsibility for your life. And I'm going to help you."

"What's lifting weights got to do with that stuff?"

"What you're good at is less important than being good at something. You got nothing. You care about nothing. So I'm going to have you be strong, be in shape, be able to run ten miles, and be able to lift more than you weigh and be able to box. I'm going to have you know how to build and cook and to work hard and to push yourself and control yourself. Maybe we can get to reading and looking at art and listening to something besides situation comedies later on. But right now I'm working on your body because it's easier to start there."

"So what," Paul said. "In a little while I'm going back. What difference does it make?"

I looked at him, white and narrow and cramped, almost birdlike, with his shoulders hunched and his head down. He needed a haircut. He had hangnails. *What an unlovely little bastard.*

"That's probably so," I said. "And that's why, kid, before you go back, you are going to have to get autonomous."

"Huh?"

"Autonomous. Dependent on yourself. Not influenced unduly by things outside yourself. You're not old enough. It's too early to ask a kid like you to be autonomous. But you got no choice. Your parents are no help to you. If anything, they hurt. You can't depend on them. They got you to where you are. They won't get better. You have to."

His shoulders started to shake.

"You have to, kid," I said.

He was crying.

"We can do that. You can get some pride, some things you like about yourself. I can help you. We can."

He cried with his head down and his shoulders hunched and the slight sweat drying on his knobby shoulders. I sat beside him without anything else to say. I didn't touch him. "Crying's okay," I said. "I do it sometimes."

In about five minutes he stopped crying. I stood

up. There were two pairs of speed gloves on top of the light bag strike board. I picked them up and offered one pair to Paul.

"Come on," I said. "Time to hit the bag."

He kept his head down.

"Come on, kid," I said. "You only got up to go. Let me show you how to punch."

Without looking up he took the gloves.

CHAPTER 18

We were digging the last hole for the foundation tubes. It was hot, the going was slow through rocks and the usual root web. I was working with a mattock and Paul had a shovel. We also had use for an ax, a crowbar, and a long-handled branch cutter, which we used on some of the roots.

Paul was dressed like I was: jeans and work boots. Mine were bigger. The sweat shone on his thin body as he dug at the dirt I loosened.

"What are these holes for again?" he said.

"See the big round cardboard tubes over there? We put them in these holes and get them level and fill them with reinforced concrete. Then we put a sill on them and the cabin rests on them. It's easier than digging a cellar hole, though a cellar's better."

"Why?" He dug the shovel blade into the dirt and picked it up. He was holding the shovel too far up the handle and the dirt flipped as he pried it up and most of it fell back in the hole.

"Cellar gives you place for a furnace, makes the floors warmer, gives you storage. This way the house sits above ground. Colder in the winter. But a lot less trouble."

Paul shifted his grip a little on the shovel and took

another stab at the dirt. He got most of it this time. "Don't they have machines to do this?"

"Yes." I swung the mattock again. It bit into the soil pleasingly. We were getting down a layer, where the roots and rocks weren't a problem. "But there's no satisfaction in it. Get a gasoline post-hole digger and rattle away at this like a guy making radiators. Gas fumes, noise. No sense that you're doing it."

"I should think it would be easier."

"Maybe you're right," I said. I swung the mattock again, the wide blade buried in the earth to the haft. I levered it forward and the earth spilled loose. Paul shoveled it out. He still held the shovel too high on the handle and he still moved too tentatively. But he cleared the hole.

"We'll use some power tools later on. Circular saws, that sort of stuff. But I wanted to start with our backs."

Paul looked at me as if I were strange and made a silent gesture with his mouth.

"It's not crazy," I said. "We're not doing this just to get it done."

He shrugged, leaning on the shovel.

"We do it to get the pleasure of making something. Otherwise we could hire someone. That would be the easiest way of all."

"But this is cheaper," Paul said.

"Yeah, we save money. But that's just a point that keeps it from being a hobby, like making ships in a bottle. Only when love and need are one, you know?"

"What's that mean?" he said.

"It's a poem, I'll let you read it after supper."

We finished the last hole and set the last tube into it. We drove reinforcing rods into the ground in each tube and then backfilled the holes around the tubes. I went around with a mason's level and got each tube upright and Paul then shoveled the earth in around it while I kept adjusting it to level. It took us the rest of the afternoon. When the last one was leveled and packed I said, "Okay, time to quit."

It was still warm and the sun was still well up in the western sky when I get a beer from the refrigerator and a Coke for Paul.

"Can I have a beer?" he said.

"Sure." I put the Coke back and got a beer.

We sat in the camp chairs with the sweat drying on our backs in the warm breeze. When the sun went down it would get cold, but now it was still the yellow-green spring of the almost deserted forest, and no human sounds but the ones we made.

"In the summer," I said, "it's much noisier. The other cabins open up and there's always people sounds."

"You like it up here?"

"Not really," I said. "Not for long. I like cities. I like to look at people and buildings."

"Aren't trees and stuff prettier?"

"I don't know. I like artifacts, things people make. I like architecture. When I go to Chicago I like to look at the buildings. It's like a history of American architecture."

Paul shrugged.

"You ever seen the Chrysler Building in New York?" I said. "Or the Woolworth Building downtown?"

"I never been to New York."

"Well, we'll go sometime," I said.

One squirrel chased another up one side of a tree and down the other and across a patch of open ground and up another tree.

"Red squirrel," I said. "Usually you see gray ones."

"What's the difference?" Paul said.

"Aside from color, gray ones are bigger," I said.

Paul was silent. Somewhere on the lake a fish broke. A monarch butterfly bobbed toward us and settled on the barrel of the shotgun that leaned against the steps to the cabin.

Paul said, "I been thinking of that stuff you said that time, about being, ah, you know, about not depending on other people."

"Autonomous," I said.

"Well, what's that got to do with building houses and lifting weights? I mean, I know what you said, but . . ." He shrugged.

"Well, in part," I said, "it's what I can teach you. I can't teach you to write poetry or play the piano or paint or do differential equations."

I finished the beer and opened another one. Paul still sipped his. We were drinking Heinekens in dark green cans. I couldn't get Amstel, and Beck's was only available in bottles. For a cabin in the woods, cans seemed more appropriate. Paul finished his beer and went and got another one. He looked at me out of the corner of one eye while he opened the new can.

"What are we going to do tomorrow?" he said.

"Anything you'd like to do?" I said. "It's Saturday."

He shrugged. If he did enough weight lifting maybe I could get him too muscle-bound to do that. "Like what?" he said.

"If you could do whatever you wanted to do, what would it be?"

"I don't know."

"When you are twenty-five, what do you imagine yourself doing?"

"I don't know."

"Is there anyplace you've always wanted to go? That no one would take you, or you were afraid to ask?"

He sipped at the beer. "I liked the movie *The Red Shoes*," he said.

"Want to go to the ballet?" I said.

He sipped at the beer again. "Okay," he said.

CHAPTER 19

It was Saturday morning.

I put on a blue suit and a white shirt from Brooks Brothers, all cotton, with a button-down collar. I had a blue tie with red stripes on it, and I looked very stylish with my black shoes and my handsome Smith & Wesson in my right hip pocket. The blue steel of the barrel was nicely coordinated with my understated socks.

Paul broke out a tan corduroy jacket and brown pants and a powder blue polyester shirt with dark blue pocket flaps. He wore his decrepit Top-Siders and no tie. His socks were black.

"That is about the ugliest goddamned getup I've seen since I came home from Korea," I said.

"I don't look okay?"

"You look like the runner-up in a Mortimer Snerd look-alike contest."

"I don't have any other stuff."

"Okay, that's what we'll do this afternoon," I said. "We'll get you some clothes."

"What will I do with these?"

"Wear them," I said. "When we get new ones you can throw those away."

"Who's Mortimer Snerd?"

"A famous ventriloquist's dummy from my youth," I said. "Edgar Bergen. He died."

"I saw him in an old movie on TV."

The ride to Boston took three and a half hours. Most of the way down Paul fiddled with the radio, switching from one contemporary music station to another as we went in and out of range of their signal. I let him. I figured I owed him for the near daily baseball games he'd listened to while we worked. We got to Boston around a quarter to twelve.

I parked Susan's Bronco on Boylston Street in front of Louis'.

"We'll go here," I said.

"Do you buy your clothes here?" he said.

"No. I don't have the build for it," I said. "They tend to the leaner pinched-waist types."

"You're not fat."

"No, but I'm sort of misshapen. My upper body is too big. I'm like a knockwurst on a canapé tray in there. The lapels don't fall right. The sleeves are too tight. Guy that's lean like you, they'll look terrific."

"You mean skinny."

"No. You were skinny. You're beginning to tend toward lean. Come on."

We went into Louis'. A slim, elegant salesman picked us up at the door.

"Yes, sir?"

He was wearing a pale gray-beige double-breasted suit with the jacket unbuttoned and the collar up, a round-collared shirt open at the neck with the blue paisley tie carefully loosened, Gucci loafers, and a lot of blue silk handkerchief showing at the breast pocket. He had a neat goatee. I decided not to kiss him.

"I'd like a suit for the kid," I said.

"Yes, sir," he said. "Come with me." If Louis' were a New York restaurant, it would be the Tavern-on-the-Green. If it were a municipality, it would be Beverly Hills. Lots of brass and oak and indirect lighting and stylish display, and thick carpet. As we got into the elevator I said softly to Paul, "I always have the impulse to whiz in the corner when I come in here. But I never do."

Paul looked startled.

"I got too much class," I said.

We bought Paul a charcoal three-piece suit of European cut, black loafers with tassels, nearly as nice as mine, two white shirts, a red-and-gray striped tie, a gray-and-red-silk pocket handkerchief, two pairs of gray over-the-calf socks, and a black leather belt. We also bought some light gray slacks and a blue blazer with brass buttons, a blue tie with white polka dots, and a blue-and-gray-silk pocket handkerchief. Under pressure they agreed to get the pants shortened for the evening. The jackets fit him decently off the rack. I offered the elegant salesman a check for seven hundred fifty dollars. He shook his head and took me to the front desk. A far less elegant young woman handled the money. The salesmen were too dignified.

"We'll have those trousers ready at five o'clock, sir."

I said thank you, and the salesman left me the clerical ministrations of the young woman.

"I'll need two pieces of identification," she said. She was chewing gum. Juicy Fruit, from the scent. I gave her my driver's license and my gumshoe permit. She read the gumshoe permit twice. We got out of the store at three ten.

"Ever been to the Museum of Fine Arts?" I said.

"No."

"We'll take a look," I said.

At the museum I offended a group being taken through by a guide. I was telling Paul something about a painting of the Hudson River School when one of the ladies in the group told us to shush.

"You're disturbing us," she said.

"Actually you're disturbing me," I said. "But I'm too well-bred to complain."

The guide looked uncomfortable. I said to Paul, "It's like a Cooper novel. The wilderness is lovely and clean. It's romantic, you know?"

The whole party glared at me in concert. Paul whispered, "I never read any novels by that guy."

"You will," I said. "And when you do, you'll think of some of these paintings."

He looked at the painting again.

"Come on," I said. "I can't hear myself think in here."

At five o'clock we picked up Paul's clothes at Louis'. The elegant salesman glided by as we did so and nodded at us democratically. We drove over to my apartment so he could change.

"Change in my bedroom," I said. "And when you get through, bring that crap out here."

"My old clothes?"

"Yes."

"Which outfit should I wear?"

"Your choice."

"I don't know what goes with what."

"The hell you don't," I said. "We picked it all out at Louis'."

"But I forgot."

"Get in there and get dressed," I said. "This is a decision you can make. I won't do it for you."

He went in and took twenty minutes to change. When he came out he was wearing the gray suit and a white shirt. He carried the red-and-gray tie. "I can't tie it," he said.

"Turn around," I said. "I have to do it backwards on you."

We stood in front of the mirror in my bathroom and I tied his tie.

"All right," I said when I ran the tie up and helped him button the collar. "You are looking good. Maybe a haircut, but for the ballet it's probably the right length."

He looked at himself in the mirror. His face was sun- and windburned, and looked even more colorful against the white shirt.

"Come on," I said. "We gotta meet Susan at Casa Romero at six."

"She's coming?"

"Yeah."

"Why does she have to come?"

"Because I love her and I haven't seen her in a couple of weeks."

He nodded.

Susan was standing on the corner of Gloucester and Newbury when we walked up. She had on a pale gray skirt and a blue blazer with brass buttons and a white oxford shirt open at the throat and black boots with very high heels. I saw her before she saw me. Her hair looked glossy in the afternoon sun. She was wearing huge sunglasses. I stopped and looked at her. She was looking for us up Newbury and we were on Gloucester.

Paul said, "What are we stopping for?"

"I like to look at her," I said. "I like to see her sometimes as if we were strangers and watch her before she sees me."

"Why?"

"My ancestors are Irish," I said.

Paul shook his head. I whistled through my teeth at Susan. "Hey, cutie," I yelled. "Looking for a good time?"

She turned toward us. "I prefer sailors," she said.

As we walked down the little alley to the entrance I gave Susan a quick pat on the backside. She smiled, but rather briefly.

It was early. There was plenty of room in the restaurant. I held Susan's chair and she sat down opposite Paul and me. The room was attractive and Aztecky with a lot of tile and, as far as I could see, absolutely no Mexicans.

We ate beans and rice and chicken *mole* and *cabrito* and flour tortillas. Paul ate a surprising amount, although he was careful to poke at each item with his fork tines first, as if to see that it was dead, and he sampled very tiny bits to make sure it wasn't poisonous. Susan had a margarita and I had several Carta Blanca beers. There wasn't much conversation. Paul ate staring into his plate. Susan responded to me mostly in short answers and while there was no anger in her voice I sensed no pleasure either.

"Suze," I said over coffee, "since I'm spending the rest of the evening at ballet. I was hoping this would be the high point."

"Did you really," she said. "Am I to gather you're disappointed?"

Paul was eating pineapple ice cream for dessert. He stared down into it as he ate. I looked at him then at Susan.

"Well, you seemed a little quiet."

"Oh?"

"I think I will pursue this, if at all, another time," I said.

"Fine," she said.

"Would you care to join us at ballet?" I said.

"I think I will not," she said. "I don't really enjoy ballet."

The waiter presented the check. I paid it.

"May we drop you somewhere?" I said.

"No, thank you. My car is just down Newbury Street."

I looked at my watch, "Well, we've got a curtain to make. Nice to have seen you."

Susan nodded and sipped her coffee. I got up and Paul got up and we left.

CHAPTER 20

I had never been to a ballet before, and while I was interested in the remarkable things the dancers could do with their bodies, I wasn't looking forward to the next time. Paul obviously was. He sat motionless and intent beside me throughout the program.

Driving back to Maine I said to him, "Ever been to a ballet before?"

"No. My dad said it was for girls."

"He's half right again," I said. "Just like the cooking."

Paul was quiet.

"Would you like to do ballet?"

"You mean be a dancer?"

"Yeah."

"They'd never let me. They think it's . . . they wouldn't let me."

"Yeah, but if they would, would you want to?"

"Take lessons and stuff?"

"Yeah."

He nodded. Very slightly. In the dark car, trying to keep an eye on the road, I barely caught the nod. It was the first unequivocal commitment I'd seen him make, and however slight the nod, it was a nod. It wasn't a shrug.

We were quiet. He hadn't turned the radio on

when he got in the car, as he almost always did. So I didn't either. Past the Portsmouth Circle, on the Spaulding Turnpike, an hour north of Boston, he said without looking at me, "Lots of men dance ballet."

"Yes," I said.

"My father says they're fags."

"What's your mother say?"

"She says that too."

"Well," I said, "I don't know about their sex life. What I can say is, they are very fine athletes. I don't know enough about dance to go much further than that, but people who do know seem to feel that they are also often gifted artists. That ain't a bad combination, fine athlete, gifted artist. It puts them two up on most people and one up on practically everybody except Bernie Casey."

"Who's Bernie Casey?"

"Used to be a wide receiver with the Rams. Now he's a painter and an actor."

There were a few streetlights and not many towns now. The Bronco moved through the night's tunnel as if it were alone.

"Why do they say that?" Paul said.

"Say what?"

"That dancing's for girls. That guys that do it are fags. They say that about everything. Cooking, books, everything, movies. Why do they say that?"

"Your parents?"

"Yes."

We went through a small town with streetlights. Past an empty brick school, past a cannon with cannonballs pyramided beside it, past a small store with a Pepsi sign out front. Then we were back in darkness on the highway.

I let some air out of my lungs. "Because they don't know any better," I said. "Because they don't know what they are, or how to find out, or what a good person is, or how to find out. So they rely on categories."

"What do you mean?"

"I mean your father probably isn't sure of whether he's a good man or not, and he suspects he might not be, and he doesn't want anyone to find out if he isn't. But he doesn't really know how to be a good man, so he goes for the simple rules that someone else told him. It's easier than thinking, and safer. The other way you have to decide for yourself. You have to come to some conclusions about your own behavior and then you might find that you couldn't live up to it. So why not go the safe way. Just plug yourself into the acceptable circuitry."

"I can't follow all that," Paul said.

"I don't blame you," I said. "Let me try another way. If your father goes around saying he likes ballet, or that you like ballet, then he runs the risk of someone else saying men don't do that. If that happens, then he has to consider what makes a man, that is, a good man, and he doesn't know. That scares the shit out of him. Same for your mother. So they stick to the tried and true, the conventions that avoid the question, and whether it makes them happy, it doesn't make them look over the edge. It doesn't scare them to death."

"They don't seem scared. They seem positive."

"That's a clue. Too much positive is either scared or stupid or both. Reality is uncertain. Lot of people need certainty. They look around for the way it's supposed to be. They get a television-commercial view of the world. Businessmen learn the way businessmen are supposed to be. Professors learn the way professors are supposed to be. Construction workers learn how construction workers are supposed to be. They spend their lives trying to be what they're supposed to be and being scared they aren't. Quiet desperation."

We passed a white clapboard roadside vegetable stand with last year's signs still up and the empty display tables dour in the momentary headlights. NATIVE CORN. BEANS. And then pine woods along the road as the headlight cone moved ahead of us.

"You're not like that."

"No. Susan says sometimes in fact I'm too much the other way."

"Like what?"

"Like I work too hard to thwart people's expectations."

"I don't get it," Paul said.

"Doesn't matter," I said. "The point is not to get hung up on being what you're supposed to be. If you can, it's good to do what pleases you."

"Do you?"

"Yeah."

"Even now?"

"Yeah."

CHAPTER 21

We ran five miles in the late May warmth and both of us glistened with sweat when we got back to the cabin. The new cabin was on the verge of beginning to look like something. The concrete pilings had cured. The sills and floor joists were down. The big plywood squares that formed the subflooring were down and trimmed. The composting toilet was in, the stool perched flagrantly on the unadorned subfloor.

"We don't lift today," Paul said. His breath was easy.

"No," I said. I took two pairs of speed gloves off the top of the speed bag strike board and gave one pair to Paul. We went first to the heavy bag. "Go ahead," I said.

Paul began to hit the bag. He still pushed his punches.

"No," I said. "Snap the punch. Try to punch through the bag." Paul punched again. "More shoulder," I said. "Turn your body and get your shoulder into it more. Turn. Turn. No, don't loop. You're hitting with the inside of your clenched hand now, on the upper parts of your fingers. Look."

I punched the bag. Jab. Jab. Hook. Jab. Jab. Hook. "Try twisting your hand as you hit. Like this, see, and extend." The bag popped and hopped as I hit it. "Like this. Punch. Extend. Twist. Extend. You try it."

Paul hit the bag again. "Okay. Now keep your feet apart like I told you. Move around it. Shuffle. Don't walk, shuffle. Feet always the same distance apart. Punch. Left. Left. Right. Right again. Left. Left. Left. Right."

Paul was gasping for breath. "Okay," I said. "Take a break." I moved in on the heavy bag and worked combinations for five minutes. Left jab, left hook, overhand right. Left jab, left jab, right hook. Then in close and I dug at the body of the bag. Short punches, trying to drive a hole through the bag, keeping the punches no more than six inches. When I stopped I was gasping for breath and my body was slick with perspiration. Paul was just getting his breath back.

"Imagine if the bag punched back," I said. "Or dodged. Or leaned on you." I said. "Imagine how tired you'd be then."

Paul nodded. "The speed bag," I said, "is easy. And showy. You look good hitting it. It's useful. But the heavy bag is where the work gets done." I hit the speed bag, making the bag dance against the backboard. I varied the rhythm, making it sound like dance steps. I whistled the "Garryowen" and hit the bag in concert with it.

"Try it," I said. "Here. You'll need this box." I put a wooden box that tenpenny nails had come in upside-down under the bag. Paul stepped up. "Hit it with the front of your fist, then the side, then the front of the other fist, then the side. Like this. I'll do it slow." I did. "Now you do it. Slow."

Paul had little success. He hit the backboard and bent over red-faced, sucking on the sore knuckles.

The box wobbled as he shifted his weight and he stepped down and kicked it, still holding his knuckles to his mouth, making a wet spot on the glove.

"You'll probably hit the swivel at least once too," I said. "That really smarts."

"I can't hit it," he said.

"It's easy to pick up. You'll be able to make it bounce pretty good in about a half hour."

It took more than a half hour, but the bag was showing signs of rhythm when it was time for lunch. We showered first. And, still damp, we sat out on the steps of the cabin and had cheddar cheese with Granny Smith apples, Bartlett pears, some seedless green grapes, and an unsliced loaf of pumpernickel bread. I had beer and so did Paul. Neither of us wore shirts. Both of us were starting to tan and signs of pectoral muscles were beginning to appear on Paul's chest. He seemed a little taller to me. Did they grow that fast?

"Were you a good fighter?" Paul said.

"Yes."

"Could you have been champion?"

"No."

"How come?"

"They're a different league. I was a good fighter, like I'm a good thinker. But I'm not a genius. Guys like Marciano, Ali, they're like geniuses. It's a different category."

"You ever fight them?"

"No. Best I ever fought was Joe Walcott."

"Did you win?"

"No."

"That why you stopped?"

"No. I stopped because it wasn't fun anymore. Too much graft, too much exploitation. Too many guys like Beau Jack who make millions fighting and end up shining shoes someplace."

"Could you beat Joe Walcott in a regular fight?"

"You mean not in the ring?"

"Yes."

"Maybe."

"Could you beat Hawk?"

"Maybe."

I drank some beer. Paul had another piece of cheese and some grapes.

"The thing is," I said, "anybody can beat anybody in a regular fight, a fight without rules. It matters only what you're willing to do. I got a gun and Walcott doesn't and poof. No contest. It doesn't make too much sense worrying about who can beat who. Too much depends on other factors."

"I mean a fair fight," Paul said.

"In a ring with gloves and rules, my fight with Walcott wasn't fair. He was much better. He had to carry me a few rounds to keep the customers from feeling cheated."

"You know what I mean," Paul said.

"Yes, but I'm trying to point out that the concept of a fair fight is meaningless. To make the match fair between me and Walcott I should have had a baseball bat. In a regular fight you do what you have to to win. If you're not willing to, you probably shouldn't fight."

Paul finished his beer. I finished mine.

"Let's start on the framing," I said.

"You can turn on the ball game if you want," Paul said.

CHAPTER 22

"You want the studs to be sixteen inches on center," I said, "so that four-by-eight sheating and stuff will fall right. You'll see when we get the walls up."

We were building the wall frames on the ground. "When we get them built we'll set them up on the platform and tie them together," I said.

"How do you know they'll fit right?" Paul said.

"I measured."

"How can you be sure your measurement is right?"

"It usually is. You learn to trust it, why wouldn't it be right?"

Paul shrugged; a gesture from the past. He began to drive a nail into one of the two-by-four studs. He held the hammer midway up the middle. His index finger was pointed along the handle toward the head. He took small strokes.

"Don't choke up on the handle," I said. "Hold it at the end. Don't stick your finger out. Take a full swing."

"I can't hit the nail that way," he said.

"You'll learn. Just like you did with the speed bag. But you won't learn if you do it that way."

He took a full swing and missed the nail altogether.

"See," he said.

"Doesn't matter. Keep at it. In a while it'll be easy. That way you let the hammer do the work."

By midafternoon we had three walls studded in. I showed Paul how to cut a length of two-by-four the proper size for a sixteen-inch on-center spacing so he didn't have to measure each time.

"What about windows?" he said as we started on the fourth wall.

"When we get the walls up, we'll frame them in, and the doors."

We were finishing up the fourth wall and getting ready to raise them when Patty Giacomin's Audi bumped in from the road and parked beside the Bronco.

When Paul saw her he stopped and stared at the car. He was wearing a hammer holster on his belt and a nailing apron tied around his waist. His bare upper body was sweaty and speckled with sawdust. There was sawdust in his hair too. As his mother got out of the car he put the hammer in its holster.

Patty Giacomin walked from her car toward us. She was awkward walking in slingback high-heeled shoes over the uncivilized ground.

"Paul," she said. "It's time to come home."

Paul looked at me. There was no expression on his face.

"Hello," she said to me. "I've come to take Paul home." To Paul she said, "Boy, don't you look grown-up with your hammer and everything."

I said, "Things straightened out between you and your husband, are they?"

"Yes," she said. "Yes, we've worked out a good compromise, I think."

Paul took his hammer out of the holster, turned,

knelt beside the wall we were studding, and began to drive a nail into the next stud.

'Paul," his mother said, "get your things. I want to get back. Spenser, if you'll bill me, I'll send you a check."

I said, "What kind of arrangement have you worked out?"

"With Mel? Oh, I've agreed to let Paul stay with him for a while."

I raised my eyebrows. She smiled. "I know, it seems like such an about-face, doesn't it?" she said. "But a boy needs a father. If it were a daughter, well, that's different."

Paul hammered at the studs, holding four or five nails in his teeth, apparently concentrating entirely on the job.

"Surprising you just thought of that," I said.

"I suppose I've been selfish," she said.

I folded my arms on my chest and pursed my lips and looked at her face.

"Paul," she said, "for heaven's sake stop that damned hammering and get your stuff."

Paul didn't look up. I looked at her face some more.

"Paul." She was impatient.

I said, "Patty. This needs some discussion."

Her head snapped around, "Now just one minute, mister. I hired you to look out for Paul, that's all. I don't need to explain things to you."

"Clever rhyme," I said.

"Rhyme?"

"*Paul* and *all*. Cute."

She shook her head shortly. I kept looking at her with my arms folded.

She said, "Why are you doing that?"

I said. "There's a credibility problem here. I'm trying to figure it out."

"You mean you don't believe me?"

"That's right," I said. "You been living with Stevie Elegant?"

"I've been staying with Stephen, yes."

"You running out of money to pay me?"

"I'll pay you what I owe you. Just send me a bill."

"But you can't afford to keep paying me."

"Not forever, of course not, who could?"

"Would you like to keep staying with the disco prince?"

"I don't see why you have to talk about Stephen that way."

"Would you?"

"I'm very fond of Stephen, and he cares for me. Yes. I'd like to share his life."

I nodded. "You want to move in with the spiffy one on a permanent basis. But he won't take the kid. You can't keep paying me to baby-sit, so you're going to ship him off to the old man."

"It's not the way you make it sound."

"So in effect your ex-husband is being asked to do you a favor. Does he know that?"

"I don't see . . ."

"He doesn't, does he? He thinks you've just been beaten down and have given up."

She shrugged.

"What do you suppose he'll do when he finds out he's doing you a favor?"

"What do you mean?"

"I mean he's spent the last six months trying to get the kid away from you because he thought you wanted to keep him and you've spent the last six months trying to keep him from getting the kid because you thought he wanted him. But he doesn't and you don't. When he finds out that you're glad he's got the kid he'll want to give him back. You'll spend the next six months trying to give him to each other."

"For God's sake, Spenser, not in front of Paul."

"Why not? You do it in front of Paul. Why shouldn't I talk about it in front of him. Neither one of you is interested in the goddamned kid. Neither one of you wants him. And both of you are so hateful that you'll use the kid in whatever way is available to hurt the other."

"That is simply not true," Patty said. Her voice sounded a little shaky. "You have no right to talk that way to me. Paul is my son and I'll decide what's best for him. He's coming home with me now and he's going to live with his father."

Paul had stopped nailing and was kneeling, his head turned toward us, listening. I looked at him. "What do you think, kid?" I said.

He shook his head.

"You want to go?" I said.

"No."

I looked back at Patty Giacomin.

"Kid doesn't want to go," I said.

"Well, he'll just have to," she said.

"No," I said.

"What do you mean?" Patty said.

"No," I said. "He's not going. He's staying here."

Patty opened her mouth and closed it. A big, fuzzy, yellow-and-black bumblebee moved in a lazy circle near my head and then planed off in a big looping arch down toward the lake.

"That's illegal," Patty said.

I didn't say anything.

"You can't take a child away from its parents."

The bee found no sustenance near the lake and buzzed back, circling around Patty Giacomin, fixing on her perfume. She shrank away from it. I batted it lightly with my open hand and it bounced in the air, staggered, stabilized, and zipped off into the trees.

"I'll have the police come and get him."

"We get into a court custody procedure and it will be a mess. I'll try to prove both of you unfit," I said. "I bet I can."

"That's ridiculous."

I didn't say anything. She looked at Paul.

"Will you come?" she said.

He shook his head. She looked at me. "Don't expect a cent of money from me," she said. Then she turned and marched back across the uneven leaf mold, wobbling slightly on her inapt shoes, stumbling once as a heel sank into soft earth. She got into the car, started up, yanked it around, and spun the wheels on the dirt road as she drove away.

Paul said, "We only got three studs to go and the last wall is finished."

"Okay," I said. "We'll do it. Then we'll knock off for supper."

He nodded and began to drive a tenpenny nail into a new white two-by-four. The sound of his mother's car disappeared. Ours was the only human noise left.

When the last wall was studded we leaned it against its end of the foundation and went and got two beers and sat down on the steps of the old cabin to drink them. The clearing smelled strongly of sawdust and fresh lumber, with a quieter sense of the lake and the forest lurking behind the big smells.

Paul sipped at his beer. Some starlings hopped in the clearing near the new foundation. Two squirrels spiraled up the trunk of a tree, one chasing the other. The distance between them remained the same as if one didn't want to get away and the other didn't want to catch it.

" 'Ever will thou love and she be fair,' " I said.

"What?"

I shook my head. "It's a line from Keats. Those two squirrels made me think of it."

"What two squirrels?"

"Never mind. It's pointless if you didn't see the squirrels."

I finished my beer. Paul got me another one. He didn't get one for himself. He still sipped at his first can. The starlings found nothing but sawdust by the foundation. They flew away. Some mourning doves came and sat on the tree limb just above the speed bag. Something plopped in the lake. There was a locust hum like background music.

"What's going to happen?" Paul said.

"I don't know," I said.

"Can they make me come back?"

"They can try."

"Could you get in trouble?"

"I have refused to give a fifteen-year-old boy back to his mother and father. There are people who would call that kidnapping."

"I'm almost sixteen."

I nodded.

"I want to stay with you," he said.

I nodded again.

"Can I?" he said.

"Yes," I said. I got up from the steps and walked down toward the lake. The wind had died as the sun settled and the lake was nearly motionless. In the middle of it the loon made his noise again.

I gestured toward him with my beer can.

"Right on, brother," I said to the loon.

CHAPTER 23

"Well, Father Flanagan," Susan said when she opened her door. "Where's the little tyke?"

"He's with Henry Cimoli," I said. "I need to talk."

"Oh, really. I thought perhaps you'd been celibate too long and stopped by to get your ashes hauled."

I shook my head. "Knock off the bullshit, Suze. I got to talk."

"Well, that's what's important, isn't it," she said. and stepped away from the door. "Coffee?" she said. "A drink? A quick feel? I know how busy you are. I don't want to keep you."

"Coffee," I said, and sat at her kitchen table by the bay window and looked out at her yard. Susan put the water on. It was Saturday. She was wearing faded jeans and a plaid shirt and no socks and Top-Siders.

"I have some cinnamon doughnuts," she said. "Do you want some?"

"Yes."

She put a blue-figured plate out and took four cinnamon doughnuts out of the box and put them on the plate. Then she put instant coffee into two blue-figured mugs and added boiling water. She put one cup in front of me and sat down across the table from me and sipped from the other cup.

"You always drink it too soon," I said. "Instant coffee's better if it sits a minute."

She broke a doughnut in half and took a bite of one half. "Go ahead," she said, "talk."

I told her about Paul and his mother. "The kid's making real progress," I said. "I couldn't let her take him."

Susan shook her head slowly. Her mouth was clamped into thin disapproval.

"What a mess," she said.

"Agreed."

"Are you ready to be a father?"

"No."

"And where does this leave us?" she said.

"Same place we've always been."

"Oh? Last time we went out to dinner it was a fun threesome."

"It wouldn't be that way all the time."

"Really? Who would guard him when we were being a twosome? Do you plan to employ Hawk as a baby-sitter?"

I ate a doughnut. I drank some coffee. "I don't know," I said.

"Wonderful," Susan said. "That's really wonderful. So what do I do while you're playing *Captains Courageous*? Should I maybe join a bridge club? Take dancing lessons? Thumb through *The Total Woman*?"

"I don't know. I don't know what you should do, or I should do. I know only what I won't do. I won't turn the kid back to them and let them play marital Ping-Pong with him some more. That's what I know. The rest has to be figured out. That's what I wanted to talk with you about."

"Oh, lucky me," Susan said.

"I did not want to talk about how you're in a funk because I'm paying more attention to him than to you," I said.

"Perhaps what you want to talk about isn't terribly important," she said.

"Yes, it is. What we have to say to each other is always important, because we love each other and we belong to each other. And will forever."

"Including what you refer to as my funk?"

"Yes."

She was silent.

"Don't be ordinary, Suze," I said. "We're not ordinary. No one else is like us."

She sat with her hands folded on the edge of the tabletop, looking at them. A small wisp of steam drifted up past her face from her coffee cup, a fleck of cinnamon sugar marred her lower lip near the corner of her mouth.

The kitchen clock ticked. I could hear a dog bark somewhere outside.

Susan put one hand out toward me and turned it slowly palm up. I took it and held it.

"There's no such thing as a bad boy," she said. "Though you do test the hypothesis."

I held her hand still and said, "First the kid wants to be a ballet dancer."

"And?"

"And I have no idea how he should go about that."

"And you think I do?"

"No, but I think you can find out."

"Aren't you supposed to be the detective?"

"Yeah, but I've got other things to find out. Can you get a handle on ballet instruction for me?"

She said, "If you'll let go of my hand I'll make some more coffee."

I did. She did. I said, "Can you?"

She said, "Yes."

I raised my coffee cup at her and said, "Good hunting." I sipped some coffee.

She said, "Assuming you can keep him despite the best efforts of both parents and the law, which rarely awards children to strangers over the wishes of the parents. But assuming that you can keep him, are you prepared to support him through college? Are you prepared to share your apartment with him? Go to P.T.A. meetings? Maybe be a Boy Scout leader?"

"No."

"No to which?"

"No to all of the above," I said.

"So?"

"So, we need a plan."

"I would say so," Susan said.

"First, I'm not sure how much the parents will want to get tangled up in legal action at the moment. Neither one wants the kid. They only wanted him to annoy each other. If they had to get into a court action to get him away from me, I'd try to prove them unfit and I might dig up things that would embarrass them. I don't know. They may each, or both, get so mad that I wouldn't give the kid up that they'll go to court, or the old man may call out his leg breakers again. Although I would think after the first two debacles they might be getting discouraged."

"Even parents who dislike their children resent giving them up," Susan said. "The children are possessions. In some cases the parents' only possession. I don't think they'll give him up."

"They don't want him," I said.

"That's not the point," Susan said. "It's a shock to

the most fundamental human condition. The sense
that no one can tell me what to do with my child. I
see it over and over in parents at school. Kids who
are physically abused by parents who were abused
when they were children. Yet the parents will fight
like animals to keep the kid from being taken away.
It's got to do with identity."

I nodded. "So you think they'll try to get him
back."

"Absolutely."

"That'll complicate things."

"And the courts will give him back. They may not
be good parents, but they aren't physically abusive.
You haven't got a case."

"I know," I said.

"If they go to the courts. As you say, the father
seems to have access to leg breakers."

"Yeah. I think about that. I wonder why."

"Why what?"

"Why he has access to leg breakers. Your average
suburban real estate broker doesn't hang out with a
guy like Buddy Hartman. He wouldn't know what
rock to look under."

"So?"

"So what kind of work has Mel Giacomin been involved in that he would know Buddy Hartman?"

"Maybe he sold him real estate, or insurance."

I shook my head. "No. Nothing Buddy's involved
in is legitimate. Buddy'd find a way to steal his insurance."

"What are you thinking?"

"I'm thinking if I can get something on Mel, and
maybe something on Patty too, I'd have some leverage to bargain with on the kid."

Susan smiled at me for the first time in some days. "Mr. Chips," she said. "Are you speaking of black-mail?"

"The very word," I said.

CHAPTER 24

I picked Paul up at the Harbour Health Club.

"He benched one-oh-five today on the Universal," Henry said.

"Not bad," I said.

Paul nodded. "The Universal is easier," he said.

"One-oh-five is one-oh-five," I said.

We walked up to the Faneuil Hall Market area and ate in Quincy Market, moving among the food stalls and collecting a large selection of food and sitting in the rotunda to eat.

"I have a plan," I said.

Paul ate part of a taco. He nodded.

"I am going to try to find out things about your parents that will let me blackmail them."

Paul swallowed. "Blackmail?"

"Not for money. Or at least not for money for me. I want to have some leverage so that I can get them off your back and off mine and maybe get you their support in what you want."

"How can you do that?"

"Well, your father knows some ugly people. I thought I might look into how come."

"Will he go to jail?"

"Would you mind if he did?"

Paul shook his head.

"Do you feel anything for him?" I said.

"I don't like him," Paul said.

" 'Course it's not that simple," I said. "You're bound to care something about his opinions, his expectations. You couldn't avoid it."

"I don't like him," Paul said.

"It's something we'll need to talk about, probably with Susan. But we don't have to do it right now." I ate some avocado-and-cheese sandwich. Paul started on his lobster roll.

"You want to help me look into this?" I said.

"About my father?"

"Yes. And your mother. We may find out things that you won't like to know."

"I don't care."

"If you help?"

"No. I don't care if I hear things about my mother and father."

"Okay. We'll do it. But remember, you probably will care. It probably will hurt. It's okay for it to hurt. It's very sensible that it should hurt."

"I don't like them," Paul said. He finished off his lobster roll.

"All right," I said. "Let's get to it."

I was parked in a slot behind the Customs House Tower by a sign that said U.S. GOVT. EMPLOYEES ONLY. As we walked to the car Paul was a few steps ahead. He'd gotten taller since I'd had him. And he was starting to fill out. He wore jeans and a dark blue T-shirt that said ADIDAS on it. His shoes were green Nikes with a blue swoosh. The hint of definition showed in his triceps at the back of his arms. And there was, I thought, a small broadening of his back as the *latissimus dorsi* developed. He walked straighter and there was some spring. He had a lot of color, reddish more than tan, as he was fair-skinned.

"You look good," I said as we got into the car.

He didn't say anything. I drove down Atlantic Avenue, across the Charlestown Bridge, and pulled up near a bar off City Square, not far from the Navy Yard. The front of the bar was done in imitation fieldstone. There was a plate glass window to the left of the doorway. In it a neon sign said PABST BLUE RIBBON. Across the window behind the neon was a dirty chintz curtain. Paul and I went in. Bar along the right, tables and chairs to the left. A color TV on a high shelf braced with two-by-fours. The Sox game was on. They were playing Milwaukee. I slid onto a barstool and nodded Paul onto the one next to me. The bartender came down the bar. He had white hair and tattoos on both forearms.

"Kid ain't supposed to sit at the bar," he said.

"He's a midget," I said, "and he wants a Coke. I'll have a draft."

The bartender shrugged and moved down the bar. He poured some Coke from a quart bottle into a glass, drew a small draft beer from the tap, and set them in front of us.

"I don't care," he said. "But it's a state law, you know."

I put a five-dollar bill on the bar. "Buddy Hartman around," I said.

"I don't know him," the bartender said.

"Sure you do," I said. "He hangs out here. He hangs out here and he hangs out at Farrell's on Rutherford Avenue."

"So?"

"So I want to give him some business." I put another five on top of the first one without looking at it.

Like I'd seen Bogie do once in a movie. The bartender took the top five, rang it up, brought me the change. He put it on the bar on top of the first five.

"He don't usually come in here till about three," he said. "Sleeps late. And he comes in here and has a fried egg sandwich, ya know." It was two twenty-five.

"We'll wait," I said.

"Sure, but the kid can't sit at the bar. Whyn't you take that table over there."

I nodded and Paul and I went to a table in the back of the bar near the door to the washroom. I left the change on the bar. The bartender pocketed it.

Paul paid no attention to the ball game, but he looked at the barroom carefully.

At two fifty Buddy Hartman strolled in, smoking a cigarette and carrying a folded newspaper. He sat on a barstool. The bartender came down the bar and said, "Guy looking for you over there. Says he's got some business."

Hartman nodded. He said, "Gimme a fried egg sandwich and a draft, will ya, Bernie?" Then he looked casually over toward me. The cigarette in his mouth drooped and sent smoke up past his left eye. He squinted his left eye against it. Then he recognized me.

He spun off the stool and headed for the door.

I said to Paul, "Come on," and went out of the barroom after him. Buddy was cutting across the expressway entry ramps, heading for Main Street.

"Watch the traffic," I said to Paul, and shifted up a gear as we crossed the ramps. Paul stayed behind me. We were both running easily. We were up to five miles a day in Maine, and I knew we'd catch Buddy all right. He was ahead, near the big pseudo-Gothic church, running erratically. He wouldn't last long.

He didn't. I caught him by the church steps with Paul close behind me. I got hold of his collar and yanked him backward and slammed his face first up against the church wall to the left of the steps. I patted him down quickly. If he had a weapon he had it well concealed.

Buddy was gasping. I let him go. He turned, coughed, and spit. His chest heaved.

"Dynamite shape, Bud," I said. "Like to see a man keep himself fit."

Buddy spit again. "Whaddya want?" he said.

"I came over to train with you, Bud. Learn some of your physical conditioning secrets."

Buddy stuck a cigarette in his mouth and lit it. He inhaled, coughed, inhaled again. "Don't fuck around with me, man. Whaddya want?"

He was in the angle between the church steps and the church wall. I had him penned so he couldn't run. His eyes kept moving past me to either side.

"I want to know how you happen to know Mel Giacomin," I said.

"Who?"

I slapped him across the face with my left hand. The cigarette flew out of his mouth in a flurry of sparks.

He said, "Hey, come on."

I said, "How do you know Mel Giacomin?"

"I seen him around, you know. I just ran into him around."

I slapped him with my right hand. His head rocked back against the wall. Buddy said, "Jesus Christ. Come on. Stop it."

"How do you know Mel Giacomin?" I said.

"He's a friend of a guy I know."

"Who's the guy?"

Buddy shook his head.

"I'm going to close my fist," I said.

"I can't tell you. He'll kill me," Buddy said.

I hit him a left hook in the side, under the last rib. He grunted and twisted.

"Him later. Me now," I said. "Whose friend is he?"

"Gimme a break," Buddy said.

I feinted another left hook and hit him in the stomach. He started to slide down the wall. I caught him and pulled him upright. He looked past me, but there was no one there. If anyone saw us, they were not getting involved.

"Who?"

"Cotton."

"Harry Cotton?"

Buddy nodded.

"How's he know Cotton?" I said.

"I don't know. Harry just told me he was a friend and wanted a favor. I don't know nothing else, honest to God."

"You doing much work for Harry?"

"Some."

"Torch?"

Buddy shook his head and flinched. "Nothing queer, Spenser, just errands." He covered his middle with his arms.

"I won't tell Harry you mentioned his name to me," I said. "I wouldn't think you'd want to either."

"I won't say nothing," Buddy said. "If he finds out, he'll have somebody burn me. Honest to God he will. You know Harry."

"Yeah. He still got that car lot on Commonwealth?"

Buddy nodded.

I turned and made a come-along gesture to Paul.

We walked down Main Street toward our car. Paul looked back once to see where Buddy was, but I didn't bother.

In the car I said to Paul, "How do you feel about that scene?"

"It scared me."

"I don't blame you. If you're not used to it, it's disturbing," I said. "In fact it's sort of disturbing even if you are used to it."

Paul was looking out the window.

"You change your mind," I said. "You want to stay with Susan for a while till I get this straightened out?"

"No. I want to go with you."

"Susan wouldn't mind," I said.

"Yes, she would," Paul said.

I didn't say anything. We went out Rutherford Avenue, across the Prison Point Bridge, and out onto Memorial Drive on the Cambridge side of the river. There were joggers on the riverbank and racing shells on the river, and a rich mix of students and old people walking along the drive. Past the Hyatt Regency I went around the circle and up onto the BU Bridge.

"Where we going?" Paul said.

"To see Harry Cotton," I said.

"He's the man Buddy said."

"Yes. He's a bad man."

"Is he a crook?"

"Yes. He's a major league crook. If your father knew him, your father was in deep."

"Are you going to do the same to him?"

"As Buddy?"

"Yes."

"I don't know. I just go along and see what happens. He's a lot harder piece of material than Buddy. You sure you want to come?"

He nodded. "There isn't anybody else," he said.

"I'm telling you , Susan . . ."

"She doesn't like me," he said. "I want to stay with you."

I nodded. "We're stuck with each other, I guess."

CHAPTER 25

Harry Cotton's car lot was up Commonwealth Avenue, near the old Braves Field, in an old gas station that no longer sold gas. There were colored lights strung around the perimeter of the lot and around the useless gas pumps. The overhead door to the repair bay was down. It had been painted with various paints in the glass panes. There was no sign to identify the business, just eight or ten lousy-looking cars without license plates jammed into the lot. There was no one on the lot. But the door to the office side of the gas station was open. I went in. Paul came in behind me.

In the office there was an old walnut desk, a wooden swivel chair, a phone, and an overhead light with a dozen dead flies inside the globe. There was an ashtray in the shape of a rubber tire full of cigarette butts on the desk. In one corner of the room a Chow with snarled hair and a gray muzzle raised his head and looked at me as I came in.

At the desk talking on the phone was Harry Cotton. Harry went with the office. He was scrawny and potbellied, with long dirty fingernails and yellow teeth. His hair was about the color of a Norway rat and parted just above his left ear. It was a lot thinner than a Norway rat's and while he tried to swoop it up and over, it didn't make it very well, and a lot of pale scalp showed through. He was smoking a menthol cigarette, which he held between the tips of his first two fingers. Apparently he always held his cigarette that way because the two fingers were stained brown from the top joint to the tip. To the right of the Chow a door opened into the maintenance bay. It was empty except for a metal barrel and three folding chairs. Three men sat on the folding chairs around the barrel playing blackjack. They were drinking Four Roses out of paper cups.

Harry hung up the phone and looked at me. He needed a shave. The stubble that showed was gray. He was wearing a red flannel shirt and over it a long-sleeved gray sweat shirt tucked into black sharkskin pants with shiny knees. His belt was too long and an extended length of it stuck out from his belt loop like a black tongue. He wore black high-top sneakers. With his feet up on the desk, his white shins showing above sagging black socks, he looked like a central casting version of Fagin and he was worth maybe three and a half million dollars.

"What do you want?" he said. The dog stood and growled. Paul moved a little more behind me.

I said, "I'm in the market for a rat farm. Everyone says you're the man to see."

"Are you trying to kid me," he said. His voice was shrill and flat.

"Me?" I said. "Kid you? A big shot like you? Not me. The boy here just asked me to define *class* and I thought it would be easier to bring him over here and show him."

The three card players in the garage looked up. One of them got up and moved to the office door. I wasn't sure he could fit through it.

"You want to get your ass kicked," Harry said, "you come to the right place. Ain't he, Shelley? Ain't he come to the right place?"

From the doorway Shelley said, "That's right. He come to the right place." Shelley looked about the same size and strength as a hippopotamus. Probably not as smart, and certainly not as good-looking. His hair was blond and wispy and hung over his ears. He wore a flowered shirt with short sleeves and his arms were smooth and completely hairless. He burped quietly and said, "Fucking anchovies."

"I'm trying to locate a guy named Mel Giacomin," I said.

"You see him here?" Harry said.

"No."

"Then buzz off."

"I heard you'd know where he is."

"You heard wrong."

"Listen up, Paul," I said. "You want to learn repartee. You're in the presence of a master."

Shelley frowned. He looked at Harry.

Harry said, "Do I know you?"

"Name's Spenser," I said.

Harry nodded. "Yeah. I know you. You're the one cleaned out Buddy Hartman and that woodchuck he brought with him a while ago."

"That's me," I said. "The woodchuck's name was Harold, I think. He had a blackjack."

Harry nodded. He was looking at me while he dragged hard on the short cigarette, making a long glowing coal reach almost to his fingers. He dropped the butt on the floor and let it smolder. He exhaled slowly, letting the smoke seep out of each corner of his mouth.

"I'm one of the guys that threw one of your people in the river off the Mass. Ave. Bridge too," I said.

Shelley was chewing tobacco. He spit tobacco juice on the floor behind him.

"What makes you think it was one of mine?" Cotton said.

"Aw, come on, Harry. We both know they were yours. We both know you're tight with Mel Giacomin and you were doing him a favor."

Harry looked at Paul. "Who's the kid?"

"He's a vice cop, undercover," I said.

"That Giacomin's kid?"

I put my hands in my hip pockets. I said, "What's your connection with Giacomin, Harry?"

"I got no connection with Giacomin," Harry said. "And I don't want you sticking your nose into my business. You unnerstand?"

"Understand, Harry. With a *D*. Un-*der*-stand. Watch my lips."

Harry's voice got a little shriller. It sounded like chalk on a blackboard.

"Shut your fucking mouth," he said. "And keep your fucking snoop nose out of my fucking business or I'll fucking bury you right here, right out front here in the fucking yard I'll bury you."

"Five," I said. "Five *fuck*'s in one sentence, Paul. That's colorful. You don't see color like that much anymore."

The other two card players were standing behind Shelley. They weren't Shelley, but they didn't look like tourists. Harry took out his handkerchief and blew his nose. He examined the results, then folded the handkerchief up and stuffed it back in his right pants pocket. Then he looked at me.

"Shelley," he said. "Throw the bum the fuck out,

and make it hurt." There was a faint touch of pink on his cheeks.

Shelley spit another batch of tobacco juice on the cement floor behind him and took a step toward me. I took my gun out of its hip holster and pointed it at him.

"Stay right there, Shelley. If I put a hole in you, the shit will seep out and you'll weigh about ninety-eight pounds."

Behind me I heard Paul breathe in.

"Harry," I said. "I can see you out of the corner of my eye. If your hands go out of sight under the desk, I'll shoot you through the bridge of your nose. I'm very good with this thing."

Everyone was still. I said, "Now what was your connection with Giacomin, Harry?"

"Go fuck yourself," Harry said.

"How about I shoot off one of your earlobes?"

"Go ahead."

"Or maybe one of your kneecaps?"

"Go ahead."

We were all quiet. The Chow had stopped growling and was sitting on his haunches with his jaw hanging and his purple tongue out. He was panting quietly.

"Paul," I said. "You see before you an example of the law of compensation. The little weasel is ugly and stupid and mean and he smells bad. But he's tough."

"You'll find fucking out how tough I am," Harry said. "You may as well stick that thing in your mouth and pull the trigger. 'Cause you're a dead man. You unnerstand that. I'm looking at a dead fucking man."

"On the other hand," I said to Paul. "I am handsome, good, intelligent, and sweet-smelling. And much tougher than Harry. Let's go."

Paul went out the door. I backed out after him. The Bronco was right in front of the station. "Go around," I said, "and go fast. Get in the other side and crouch down."

He did what I told him and I followed, backing, my gun steady at the open door. Then we were in the car and out of the lot, and heading toward Brighton on Commonwealth Avenue.

Beside me Paul was very white. He swallowed several times, audibly.

"Scary," I said.

He nodded.

"Scared me too," I said.

"Did it really?" he said.

"Sure. Still does. But there's nothing to be done about it. Best just to go ahead with your program. Being scared is normal, but it shouldn't change anything."

"You didn't seem scared."

"Best not to," I said.

"Why would he let you shoot him? If he's doing something with my father, he must really want to keep it quiet."

"Maybe. Or maybe he's just stubborn. Won't be pushed. He didn't get to be as big a deal in this town as he is by being a piece of angel cake. Even garbage has pride sometimes. Maybe you need to have more if you're garbage."

I U-turned where Commonwealth curves off toward BU and headed back downtown.

"What did you get out of that?" Paul asked.

"Found out a little," I said.

"What?"

"Found out that your father's connection to Harry Cotton is worth covering up."

"Maybe that other guy was lying," Paul said.

"Buddy? No. If he lied, it wouldn't be like that. If Cotton ever heard that Buddy had fingered him, he'd have Buddy killed. Buddy would lie to get out of trouble. But not that way."

"If that guy Cotton is so rich and everything," Paul said, "why is he so junky?"

"I suppose he figures it doesn't attract attention," I said. "Maybe he's just thrifty. I don't know. But don't let it fool you."

"What are we going to do now?"

"Your father have an office set up at his apartment?"

"Yes."

"We're going to burgle it."

CHAPTER 26

Paul and I spent the night in my apartment in Boston. And the next morning about ten thirty we broke into his father's apartment in Andover. There was no one home. Like all the other good suburban business types, Mel Giacomin was out laying nose to grindstone.

"His office is in back where I slept when I was here," Paul said.

Through the dining room with the kitchen opening to the right and down a very short hall there were two bedrooms and a bath. Mel wasn't a neat guy. The breakfast dishes were still laying around the kitchen. Coffee for one, I noticed, and a Rice Krispies box. A health food addict. Mel's bed in the right-hand bedroom was unmade and there were dirty clothes on the floor. There were wet towels on the bathroom floor. The other door was closed and locked with a padlock. I stepped as far back as the narrow hall would let me, raised my right foot, and kicked the door with the flat of my foot. The padlock hasp tore loose from the wood. We went in. The office was neat. There was a studio couch. A table that once functioned in a kitchen, a straight chair, and a two-drawer metal file with a lock. On the table were a phone, a lamp, a beer mug holding pencils and pens, and a card file. The card file was locked too. There was a small Oriental rug on the floor, an air conditioner in the room's one window, and nothing else.

"Let's just take the files," I said. "Simpler than breaking them open and going through them here."

"But won't he know?"

"He'll already know I kicked in his door. I don't care if he knows that someone took his files. If he thinks it's me, fine. If there's things in here to make him nervous, maybe he'll make a move. If he does, things will happen. That's a plus. You take the card file."

And out we went. Paul with the card file, and me wrestling the bigger file. "It's not heavy," I said. "It's just awkward."

"Sure," Paul said. "That's what they all say."

We loaded the files in the back of the Bronco and drove away. No one yelled at us. No policemen blew their whistles. I'd learned over the years that if you're not wearing a mask you can walk in and out of almost anywhere and carry away almost anything and people assume you're supposed to.

I parked in the alley in back of my office and Paul and I carried the files up. It had been a while since I'd been in my office. There was a batch of mail on the floor below the mail slot. A spider had made a web in one corner of my window. Since it didn't interfere with my view of the ad agency across the street, I left it alone.

I put the big file down next to my desk. Paul put the card file on top of it. I opened the window and picked up my mail and sat at my desk to read it. Most of it went right to the wastebasket unopened. What was left was a copy of a book autographed by the woman who'd written it, a woman I'd done some work for awhile ago, and an invitation to attend the wedding of Brenda Loring to someone named Maurice Kerkorian. Reception following the ceremony at the Copley Plaza Hotel. I looked at the invitation for a long time.

"What are we going to do with these files?" Paul said.

I put the mail down. "After we get them open we'll look and see what's there."

"What are we looking for?"

"Don't know. We'll see what's there."

"What did you mean it would be good if my father knew you'd taken the files?" Paul said.

I got a pinch bar out of the coat closet in the corner of the office and began to pry the file drawers open.

"Gets him moving. The worst thing that can happen if you're trying to find out about people is to have them hunker down and stay put. If they simply sit on whatever it is and do nothing, then nothing happens. They don't commit themselves, don't give you a chance to counterpunch, don't make mistakes, don't open themselves up, if you follow."

"What do you think my father might do?"

"He might try to get the files back."

"And what if he does?"

"We'll see."

"But you don't know?"

The last file drawer snapped open under the pressure of the bar. "No, I don't know. But if you'll excuse the phrase, it's the way life is. You don't know what's going to happen. People whose lives work best are the ones who recognize that and, having done what they can, are ready for what comes. Like the man said, 'Readiness is all.'"

"What man?"

"Hamlet."

"That's what you did with Harry."

"Yeah, partly. You go from handle to handle. I tried Buddy, and then Harry, and now your father. It's like walking down a long corridor with a bunch of doors. You keep trying them to see which one opens. You don't know what's behind the doors, but if you don't open any, you don't get out of the corridor."

"All that's in this card file are a bunch of names," Paul said.

I took a card and looked at it. It said *Richard Tilson. 43 Concord Avenue. Waltham. Whole Life. 9/16/73. Prudential #3750916.* "Client file, I guess," I said. I looked at some other cards. Same setup. "Run through them," I said. "Make a note of any names you know. Make sure it's all client information."

"Why do you want me to list people I know?"

"Why not? Might matter. It's a thing to do with the file. Maybe a pattern will crop up. You won't know till you've done it."

I gave Paul a pad and pencil from my desk and he sat in my client's chair with the file on his side of my desk and began to go through it. I turned on the portable radio to a contemporary sound station for Paul and began to go through the contents of the big file on my side of the desk. It was slow. There was correspondence to be read, all of it couched in the clotted, illiterate jargon of economic enterprise. After ten minutes I was getting cerebral gas pains. The music wasn't helping. "If Andy Warhol were a musician, he'd sound like this," I said.

Paul said, "Who's Andy Warhol?"

"It's better you should not know," I said.

At one thirty I tuned to the ball game. Relief. At two I said to Paul, "You hungry?"

"Yeah."

"Why don't you walk over to that sandwich shop on Newbury and get us some food."

"Where is it?"

"Just a block down and around the corner. Right across from Brooks Brothers."

"Okay."

I gave him some money. "Get whatever looks good," I said.

"What do you want?"

"Use your own judgment," I said.

"Okay."

He went out and I kept at the files. Paul came back with turkey sandwiches on oatmeal and roast beef sandwiches on rye and two lemon turnovers and a carton of milk. I had coffee from the coffee pot. By three Paul had finished with his file. He said, "I'm going to walk around."

I said, "You need any money?"

He said, "No. I still got change from what you gave me before."

At five Paul came back. He'd bought a book on ballet at the Booksmith up Boylston.

He read his book while I worked on the files. It got dark. I turned on the lights in the office. At eight fifteen I said, "Enough. Come on, I'll buy you dinner."

We went up to Café L'Ananas and ate. I got a bottle of wine and Paul had some. Then we walked back to my apartment. "What about your car?" Paul said.

"We'll leave it there. It's only a four-block walk to my office."

"We going back tomorrow?"

"Yeah, I'm not through."

"I only found three people on the list."

"More than I've found so far."

We went upstairs and went to bed.

CHAPTER 27

It was nearly noon the next day before I found anything. It wasn't a bloody dagger or even an Egyptian dung beetle sculptured from gold. It was a list of addresses. It wasn't much, but it was all there was. It was on a single sheet of paper by itself in an unlabeled file folder in the back of the bottom file drawer.

"What's important about that?" Paul said.

"I don't know, but it's the only thing that doesn't have a simple explanation."

I got a city directory out of the bottom drawer of my desk and thumbed through it, looking up the names of the people at the addresses. The fourth one I looked up was Elaine Brooks.

"Isn't Elaine Brooks your father's girl friend?"

"Yes."

"This isn't where she lives."

Paul said, "I don't know where she lives."

"I do. I followed her to you, remember?"

"Maybe she used to live there."

"Maybe."

"She's on my list," he said.

"From the card file?"

"Yes."

"Let me see this list."

He gave it to me. There were two other names

besides Elaine Brooks. I consulted the city directory. Both the names were listed in the city directory as owning property at one or another address on the list. Elaine Brooks owned two addresses.

"The card file alphabetical?"

Paul said, "Yes."

"Okay. I'm going to read you some names. You look them up and see if they are in your file. If they are, pull the card and give me the address."

I went through the whole list of addresses, looking each up in the city directory and giving Paul the name I found. All of them were in the file. None of them were listed on the cards at the address in the city directory. "What kind of insurance is listed?" I said when we were through and all the cards were pulled.

"This one says casualty."

"Yeah?"

"This one says homeowner's."

"Any of them say life?"

Paul ruffled through the cards. "No," he said.

I took the cards and made a master list of names and both addresses and the kinds of insurance each had. All had casualty. Everyone was insured with a different company. When I was through, I said to Paul, "Let's go take a look at this property."

The first address was on Chandler Street in the south end. The south end was once rather elegant redbrick town houses. Then it fell into slum wino. Now it was coming back. A lot of upper-middle-class types were moving in and sandblasting the bricks and buying Dobermans and installing alarm systems and keeping the winos at bay. It was an interesting mix: black street kids; winos of many races; white women in tapered pants and spike heels; middle-aged men, black and white, in Lacoste shirts. Our address was between a soul-food takeout and a package store. It was burned out.

" 'Bare ruined choirs,' " I said, " 'Where late the sweet birds sang.' "

"Frost?" Paul said.

"Shakespeare," I said. "Why'd you think it was Frost?"

" 'Cause you always quote Frost or Shakespeare."

"Sometimes I quote Peter Gammons," I said.

"Who's he?"

"The *Globe* baseball writer."

We drove to the next address on Symphony Road in the Back Bay. Symphony Road was students and what the school board called Hispanics. The address was a charred pile of rubble.

"Bare ruined church," Paul said.

"Choirs," I said. "Do we sense a pattern developing?"

"You think they'll all be burned?"

'Sample's a little small," I said, "but the indices are strong."

The third address was on Blue Hill Avenue in Mattapan. It was between a boarded-up store and a boarded-up store. It had burned.

"Where are we?" Paul said.

"Mattapan."

"Is that part of Boston?"

"Yes."

"God, it's awful."

"Like a slice of the South Bronx," I said. "Life is hard here."

"They're all going to be burned," Paul said.

'Yeah, but we gotta look."

And we did. We looked in Roxbury and Dorchester

and Allston and Charlestown. In Hyde Park and Jamaica Plain and Brighton. The addresses were always obscure so that we sometimes crisscrossed the same neighborhoods several times, following our list. All the addresses were in unpretentious neighborhoods. All had been burned. It was dark when we got through, and a little rain was starting to streak my office windows.

I put my feet up on my desk and shrugged my shoulders, trying to loosen the back muscles that eight hours of city driving had cramped. "Your daddy," I said, "appears to be an arsonist."

"Why would he burn all those buildings down?"

"I don't know that he burned them. He may have just insured them. But either way it would be for money. Buy it, burn it, collect the insurance. That's his connection to Cotton. Your old man's business was real estate and insurance. Cotton's is money and being bad. Put them together and what have you got?"

"Bibbity-bobbity-boo," Paul said.

"Oh, you know the song. How the hell could you?"

"I had it on a record when I was little."

"Well, it fits. And then when your father needed a little cheap sinew to deal with his divorce situation, Cotton sent him Buddy Hartman and Hartman brought Harold and his musical blackjack."

"What will you do now?" Paul said.

"Tomorrow I'm going to call up all these insurance companies and find out if your father was in fact the broker on these fire losses, and if they paid off."

"The ones in the card file?"

"Yeah."

"How will you know who to call?"

"I've done a lot of work for insurance companies. I know people in most of the claims departments."

"Then what will you do?"

"Then I'll file all of what I know for the moment and see what I can get on your mother."

Paul was quiet.

"How do you feel?" I said.

"Okay."

"This is awful hard."

"It's okay."

"You're helping me put the screws to your father and mother."

"I know."

"You know it's for you?"

"Yes."

"Can you do it?"

"Help you?"

"All of it. Be autonomous, be free of them, depend on yourself. Grow up at fifteen."

"I'll be sixteen in September."

"You'll be older than that," I said. "Let's get something to eat and go to bed."

CHAPTER 28

It was raining hard in the morning when Paul and I ran along the Charles River. It rained all day. I sat in my office and called insurance companies. Paul had finished his book on ballet. He went out and, at my suggestion, walked up to the Boston Public Library and used my card to take out a copy of *Catcher in the Rye*. Five minutes after he was back, Susan called.

"The line's been busy for an hour," she said.

"Broads," I said. "Word's out that I'm back in town and the broads have been calling since yesterday."

"Paul with you?"

"Yes."

"Let me speak to him, please."

I held the phone out to Paul. "For you," I said. "Susan."

Paul took the phone and said, "Hello."

Then he was quiet.

Then he said, "Okay."

Then he was quiet.

Then he said, "Okay," and hung up.

"She says there's a prep school out in Grafton that specializes in drama, music, and dance," he said. "She says she'll take me out to look at it this afternoon if I want to go."

"You want to go?"

"I guess so."

"Good. You should. Is it a boarding school?"

"You mean live there?"

"Yes."

"She didn't say. Would I have to live there?"

"Maybe."

"You don't want me to live with you?"

"Eventually you'll have to move on. Autonomy means self-reliance, not changing your reliance from your mother and father to me. I'm what they call in politics a transition coordinator."

"I don't think I want to go away to school."

"Wait, see, take a look at the place. We'll talk. I won't make you do what you genuinely can't stand to do. But keep open. Keep in mind that sometimes I go to unpleasant places and people shoot at me. There are drawbacks to living with me."

"I don't mind."

"Some of the drawbacks might be mine," I said.

"Oh."

"Don't make more of that than it is. If one of us starts fearing that honesty will hurt the other's feelings, we've slid back some. I'm trying to work this out so it's best for all of us, me as well as you. Susan too."

He nodded.

"I've taken you this far. I won't push you out of the nest until we both know you can fly. You understand that?"

"Yes."

"You can trust me to do what I say. Do you know that?"

"Yes."

"Okay. Willing to make another trip out in the rain?"

"Yes."

"I'm in a Dunkin' Donut frenzy," I said. "If you went up Boylston Street and bought some, and coffee to go, and hurried back before the coffee got cold, I might be able to make it until afternoon."

He grinned. "Since I've known you you've been a health food freak."

I gave him five dollars. He put on the yellow slicker jacket I'd bought him and left.

I called a guy in Chicago named Flaherty at Colton Insurance Company of Illinois. He told me that they had insured property in the name of Elaine Brooks, that six months later the building burned, and that while everyone guessed it was arson, no one could prove it and they paid and privately agreed not to insure Elaine again.

"Thing is," he said, "if it was arson, it was also murder. Two winos were apparently cooping up in there and never got out. What they found was mostly charred bones and a muscatel bottle that had half melted."

I said, "Thanks, Jack," and noted the information on my master list.

He said, "You got anything I should know about on this thing, Spenser?"

"No, I'm into something else, this is just collateral, you know."

"Well, don't hold out on us. I throw a lot of investigative work your way."

"Yeah, and it's real exciting too," I said.

"Don't knock it, money's good."

"Money's not everything, Jack," I said.

"Maybe not, but you ever try spending sex?"

"There's something wrong with that argument," I said, "but I can't think what right now. I may call you later with my comeback."

"Keep in touch," Flaherty said.

We hung up. Murder, two counts. Better and better. Or worse and worse, depending on where you stood. From where I stood it looked like enough to keep Mel Giacomin in line.

Paul came back with coffee and doughnuts. Plain for me. Two Boston creams for him—disgusting. I made some more of my calls. Everything was clicking in. Giacomin was involved with some kind of arson ring, and there was no doubt, though at the moment, no proof, that Harry Cotton was in it with him.

Susan showed up in the MG at two thirty. She had on a soft felt hat with a big floppy brim and a brass ring on the hatband. She also wore a light leather trench coat and high-heeled boots of the same color. I wished I were going to look at ballet schools with her. "This will be the real test," I said to Susan. "If the instructional staff doesn't attempt to seduce you *en masse* it will prove they're gay."

She wrinkled her nose at me. "I'll tell them how big and tough you are," she said. "Maybe they'll hesitate long enough for us to escape."

Paul said, "What if they attempt to seduce *me*?"

I grinned. "That would be further proof, I think."

They left and I finished up my phone calls. There were no surprises.

I made the final notes on my master sheet and then got out some fresh bond paper and typed it all out neatly and went out to a copy shop and had two copies made and came back and filed the original in my office. I mailed the second one to myself at my apartment and stuck the third copy in my pocket for handy reference. Also maybe for showing to Mel Giacomin along with threats. I looked at my watch. Four twenty. I had to get away from the desk.

I locked up the office, got into the Bronco, and cruised down to the waterfront. Henry Cimoli was sitting behind the office desk in the Harbour Health Club in white pants, sneakers, and a white T-shirt. He looked like the world's toughest jockey. He had in fact been one of the best lightweight fighters around and gone fifteen rounds once and lost a split decision to Willie Pep. His arms bulged against the T-shirt and his short body moved like a compressed spring, a great deal of contained energy.

"Come to try and rescue what's left, kid?" he said.

"Yeah. You think it's too late?"

"Almost."

I went to my locker and changed. In the exercise room there were weight machines, barbells, dumbbells, a heavy bag, two speed bags. The walls were mirrored. I started working on bench presses.

I was almost through my workout when Hawk came in at about seven. He wore silky-looking warmup pants with the bottoms unzipped, and high white boxer's shoes and no shirt. He had a pair of speed gloves in the hip pocket of the warmup pants and he carried a jump rope. Most of the people in the room eyed him covertly. He nodded at me, did a few stretching exercises, and began to jump rope. He jumped rope for a half hour, varying the step and speed, crisscrossing the rope.

As he finished I started on the speed bag. He hung the rope up and came over beside me and started on the other bag. As I began to get a rhythm down on the bag he began to punch in counterpoint. I grinned and started to whistle "Sweet Georgia Brown."

He nodded and picked up the beat. We began to alternate, picking up the pace. Like a battle of two drummers from the forties. Hawk picked up the tempo, I picked it up a little more. Hawk used his elbows and fists. I alternated one hand then the other. People began to group around us and the rhythm of the bag and the sense of competition began to carry me. I concentrated as the bag was a wine-colored blur in time with Hawk's. We did paradiddles and rolls, and some of the men in the exercise room cheered at one or another of us. Then they began to clap in rhythm to the bags and Hawk and I carried them with us until the place was in an uproar and Henry came in from the front desk and yelled at Hawk, "Telephone."

Hawk did shave-and-a-haircut-two-bits on his bag and I responded and we stopped, and Hawk, grinning widely, went to the phone. The rest of the room cheered and clapped. I yelled after him.

"Hey, gee whiz, my dad's got a barn, maybe we can put on a show."

Hawk disappeared around the corner and I went to the heavy bag. When he came back his grin wasn't as wide, but his face had a look of real pleasure.

He leaned on the other side of the bag while I pounded it.

"You going to like this, babe," he said.

"You been drafted," I said.

"You been messing with Harry Cotton, haven't you?"

I dug a hook into the bag. "I spoke with him."

"You got that slick way, you know, how you talk so sweet to people. Harry putting out a hit on you."

"He's too sensitive," I said. "Call a guy a weasel

and tell him he smells bad and he goes right into a goddamned swivet," I said.

"He do smell bad, that's a fact," Hawk said.

"You know Harry?"

"Oh, yes. Harry's an important person in this town."

"That him on the phone?"

"Yeah. He want me to whack you." Hawk's smile got wider. "He ask me if I know who you are. I say, yeah, I think so."

I did a left jab and an overhand right.

"How much he offering?" I said.

"Five G's."

"That's insulting," I said.

"You'd have been proud of me," Hawk said. "I told him that. I said I wouldn't do it for less than ten. He say lot of people be happy to do it for five. I said that wasn't the point. I said lot of people be happy to do it for nothing, but they can't, 'cause they ain't good enough. I said it's a ten-thousand-dollar job at least. He say no."

"Harry was always cheap," I said.

"So I said no. Guess you safe again."

"From you at least." I did some low body punches into the bag. Hawk held it steady.

"Harry will hire cheap," Hawk said. "He'll hire some bum, don't know no better. You'll bury him and . . ." Hawk spread his hands. "I got nothing going for a while. Maybe I hang around with you some."

"What would the rate for hitting us both be?" I said.

" 'Bout one hundred and thirty-two trillion," Hawk said.

"Harry's too cheap for that," I said.

CHAPTER 29

At nine o'clock I was at the Giacomin house in Lexington. I forced the back door and went in and turned on the lights. In Patty Giacomin's bedroom was a small secretary with slender curving legs and gold stenciling. Her picture in a leather frame was on it. I opened the leaf and sat down on the small rush-bottomed stool in front of it and began to go through the contents. When I'd been here I'd seen Patty do her bills here, and there wasn't much else but bill-payment receipts and canceled checks. The only handle I had besides her sweet Stephen was her periodic trips to New York.

In a half hour I found what I wanted: American Express receipts from the New York Hilton dated roughly a month apart going back several years. They were all room charges, she'd paid them all with her American Express card, and she'd kept the receipts. She kept all receipts apparently without discrimination. So there was nothing terribly significant about her keeping these. She probably didn't know what was important, so she kept them all.

I went through everything else in the house and there was nothing else worth looking at. I took all the American Express receipts and Patty's picture, turned off the lights, and closed the door.

The spring night was quiet in Lexington. The rain had stopped. Lights shone in people's houses and there were open windows. Voices drifted out occasionally, and the sounds of television. It was late, but there were still cooking smells in the air. As I went toward my car, a cat slid past me and into the shrubs in the next yard. I thought about Harry Cotton's contract. I touched the gun on my hip. The street, when I got to the car, was empty. In the circle of the streetlights moths flew without apparent purpose. The cat appeared from the shrubs and sat on its haunches under the streetlight and looked up at the moths. It was a yellow-striped cat with white chest and face and paws.

I got into the Bronco and started up and drove away from Emerson Road. The ball game was coming in from Milwaukee and it made the sound it always made, soft crowd murmur in the background, the voices of the announcers in familiar pattern, the occasional sound of the bat hitting the ball, the metallic stilted voice of the P.A. announcer, repeating the hitter's last name. The sound seemed almost eternal.

It was nearly midnight when I got back to my apartment. Susan and Paul were still up watching a movie on television. Susan said, "There's a sub out there if you haven't eaten."

I got the sandwich and a beer and came back into the living room. The movie was *An American in Paris*. "How was the Laurel School?" I said.

"The admissions guy was a feeb," Paul said.

I looked at Susan. She nodded. "Regrettable but true," she said. "Everything you hoped he wouldn't be."

"Effeminate?"

"Effeminate, affected, supercilious," Susan said.

"Susan yelled at him," Paul said. His eyes were bright.

I looked at Susan. "He was a pompous little twerp," she said.

"Is he now aware of that?" I said.

"That's what she told him," Paul said.

"Did he get scared?" I said.

Susan said, "I think so."

"Well," I said. "It can't be the only school in the world."

There was an extended dance scene on the television screen. Paul watched it closely. We were quiet while I finished the sub and the beer. I went to the kitchen and put the can in the wastebasket and the plate in the dishwasher. I washed my hands and face at the kitchen sink and came back into the livingroom. There was a commercial on the tube.

I said to Paul, "You ever been to New York?"

He said, "No."

"Want to go tomorrow?"

"Okay."

"How about you, sugarplum?" I said to Susan.

"I've been," she said.

"I know," I said. "Want to go again?"

"Yes."

I felt the softening of relief and pleasure in the area of my diaphragm.

"We'll hit the shuttle, bright and early."

"Bright maybe," Susan said, "but not too early. I have to call in sick and I have to pack."

"We'll go when you're ready, my love," I said.

And the next day we did. We got the one o'clock shuttle from Logan to LaGuardia. I had my stuff and Paul's in a single suitcase. Susan had two. As I drove to the airport I noticed Hawk's silver Jag parked outside my house. It followed me to the airport garage and as I turned in, it drove by and headed out the exit road. Neither Susan nor Paul noticed. I didn't remark on it.

We got into New York at about one thirty and into the New York Hilton at about two fifteen. We got adjoining rooms. Paul and me in one, Susan in the other. The New York Hilton is big and conveniently located on Sixth Avenue. It is efficient, flossy, and as charming as an electric razor.

Paul was looking out the window of the hotel, staring down into Fifty-fourth Street far below. I remembered the first time I'd come to New York. I'd come with my father at about Paul's age. My father had brought me to go to ball games and tour Rockefeller Center and eat in an Italian restaurant he knew of. He'd pinned half his money to his undershirt in the hotel room, and put the other half back into his wallet. I remembered his grin when he pinned the money to his undershirt. Always tell a country boy, he'd said. I remembered the smell of the city and the sound of it, and the sense of it boiling at all hours, and almost always the sound of a siren somewhere at the edge of the sound. I had stood as Paul was standing, staring out. I'd never seen anything like it. And since then I never have.

I went through the connecting door into Susan's room. She was carefully hanging her clothes up.

I said, "Have you ever noticed what happens to me when I enter a hotel room?"

She said, "Yes. Actually it seems to happen in the elevator going up to the hotel room. But what are we going to tell Paul?"

"Maybe later," I said. "The little fella has to sleep sometime, doesn't he?"

"Let us hope so," Susan said. "Now that we're here, what are we here for?"

"I want to look into Patty Giacomin. She came here about once a month and stayed overnight. It's all I could find that seemed in any way unusual. I thought I'd ask around."

She looked at her watch. "Do you think Paul would care for a tour of Radio City?"

"I would think so," I said. "Can you stand to take him?"

"Yes."

"Thank you."

She smiled. "You're welcome. If he's very tired tonight, he may go to sleep early."

I nodded.

"Do you suppose they have champagne on the room service menu?" she said.

"They better," I said.

Her clothes were all hung up. She was very careful with them. She checked herself in the mirror, made an unidentifiable adjustment to her hair, went to the other room and said, "Come on, Paul. We'll go for a mystery walk."

"What's that?" Paul said.

"You'll find out," Susan said.

Paul opned the door. Susan paused in it and said to me, "I want the Four Seasons," she said.

"Tonight," I said. "It's yours."

When they were gone I madc the reservation and then took Patty's picture and went down to the lobby. There was an assistant manager's desk near the elevator bank. The assistant manager was behind it, in a three-piece black pinstripe suit and a pink shirt with a pin collar. I took my license out and placed it on the desk in front of him. He read it without expression. Then he looked at me. "Yes?" he said.

"Who's your security man and/or woman as the case may be?"

"What can we do for you?"

"Gee," I said. "The sign says assistant manager."

"A harmless euphemism," he said. He had receding hair and a neat mustache and good color. I noticed that his hands were manicured and his fingernails were buffed. "Euphemism?" I said. "What kind of security person says euphemism?"

"I was a cop in this city for twenty-two years, sailor. You want to try me out."

I shook my head. "Not me," I said, "I need to find out about this lady here."

I showed him Patty Giacomin's picture.

"In what context?" the assistant manager said.

Trying to explain what I was doing was too complicated. "She's missing," I said. "Husband's worried. Asked me to come down and look."

"She stayed here overnight about once every month," I said. "Last time was about three weeks ago."

"She's not here now?"

"No." I said, "I already checked."

He looked at me for a moment. His shaving lotion was strong and expensive. "You got somebody to vouch for you?" he said. "I don't like talking hotel business with every jerk that comes in here and waves a license at me."

"I liked you better when you were saying things like *euphemism*," I said.

"I don't care what you like. You got somebody to vouch for you?"

"How about Nicky Hilton?"

He almost smiled. "Best you can do?"

"Look at me in profile," I said. "Could I be anything but trustworthy?"

He heaved a sigh. "Come on," he said. He came out from behind the desk and we walked down the lobby to a cocktail lounge. It was almost empty at three in the afternoon. The bartender was a tall trim black man with a tight Afro and big handlebar mustache. The assistant manager gestured him down the bar with his head.

"What'll it be, Mr. Ritchie," the bartender said.

Assistant Manager Ritchie said, "Jerry, you know this babe?" I held up the picture of Patty Giacomin. Jerry looked at it carefully, his hazel eyes expressionless. He looked at Ritchie.

Ritchie said, "Tell him, Jerry. He's okay."

"Sure," Jerry said, "I know her. She comes in here about once a month, gets fried on Chablis, picks up a guy, and goes out with him. To her room, I assume."

Ritchie nodded. "Yeah, to her room. Next day she checks out, pays her bill, and we don't see her for a month."

"Different guy each time?" I said.

"Yeah. I guess so," Jerry said. "Couldn't swear there was never somebody twice, but if it was, it was an accident. She was in here to get laid. She didn't care who."

"Know any of the guys?" I said.

Jerry looked at Ritchie. Ritchie said, "No."

"And if you did?" I said.

"I wouldn't tell you," Ritchie said.

"Unless I come back with somebody from your old outfit," I said.

"Come back with a New York cop on a missing person's investigation, we'll spill our guts. Otherwise, you have found out all you're going to."

"Maybe enough," I said.

CHAPTER 30

We had dinner at the Four Seasons, in the pool room, under the high ceiling near a window on the Fifty-third Street side. Paul had pheasant, among other things, and paid very close attention to everything Susan and I did. We had some wine, and the bill came to $182.37. I have bought cars for less. The next day we went to the Metropolitan Museum in the afternoon and in the evening we took Paul up to Riverside Church to see Alvin Ailey and his group dance.

In the cab going back downtown Paul said, "That's not exactly ballet, is it?"

"Program says contemporary dance," I said.

"I like that too."

"There are surely lots of variations," Susan said, "Tap dance too."

Paul nodded. He stared out the cab window as we went down the West Side Highway and off at Fifty-seventh Street. We were alone, the three of us, going up in the hotel elevator and Paul said, "I want to learn. I'm going to learn how to do that. If I have to go away to school or whatever. I'm going to do that."

Sunday we slept late and in the early afternoon went up to Asia House and looked at nineteenth-century photographs of China. The faces looking back at us from 130 years were as remote and unknowable as patterns on another planet, and yet there they were; human and real, maybe feeling at the moment the shutter clicked a rolling of the stomach, a stirring of the loins.

We took a late-afternoon shuttle back to Boston and drove Susan out to her house. It was after six when we got there. I pulled the Bronco in next to my MG and parked and ran the back window down with the lever on the dash. Susan and Paul got out on their side, I got out on mine. As we walked back to get the luggage, I heard a car engine kick in. I looked up and a 1968 Buick was rolling down the street toward us. The barrel of a long gun appeared in the window. I jumped at Paul and Susan, got my arms around both of them, and took them to the ground with me on top, scrambling to get us all behind the car. The long gun made the urgent bubbling sound an automatic weapon makes and slugs ripped into the sheet metal of the Bronco and then passed and the Buick was around the corner and gone before I could even get my gun out.

"Lay still," I said. "They could make a U-turn." I had the gun out now and crouched behind the engine block. The car didn't come back and the street was quiet again. The neighbors didn't even open a door. Probably didn't know what they'd heard. Automatic fire doesn't sound like a gunshot.

"Okay," I said. "Let's unpack."

Susan said, "Jesus Christ," as she got up. The front of her dress was littered with grass blades and small leaves. Paul didn't say anything, but he stayed close to me as we carried the bags into the house.

"What was that about?" Susan said in her kitchen.

"I annoyed a guy," I said. "Probably Harry Cotton, Paul."

Paul nodded.

"Who's Harry Cotton?" Susan said. She was making coffee.

"Guy that Mel Giacomin did business with."

"And why is he shooting at you, and, incidentally, us?"

"I have been looking into the relationship between Harry and Mel Giacomin. And Harry doesn't like it."

"Are we going to call the police?"

"No."

"Why not?"

"It would blow what I'm working on."

"Maybe you'd better tell me in more detail what you're working on," Susan said. "Since it seems to be getting me shot at."

"Okay," I said. "You know I have been trying for some purchase on Paul's parents so I could get them off his back."

"Blackmail," Susan said.

"Yes. Well, I've got it. I can produce a batch of evidence that Mel Giacomin was involved in a major arson scheme to burn down buildings for the insurance. He was in it with Harry Cotton, who's a big-league bad person in town. I can't prove Harry's part, but if I give what I've got to Marty Quirk, it's only time till the fuzz can. So I got something fairly heavy on Mel. To get it I've had to lean on some people including Harry Cotton and he's mad at me. He put out a contract."

"To kill you?" Susan said.

"Yes, he's employed people to kill me."

"How do you know?" Paul said.

"He tried to hire Hawk," I said.

"Aren't you scared?" Paul said.

"Yes. But like I said, there's nothing to be done about that, so I don't spend much time thinking about it."

"I'm scared," Susan said.

"Me too," Paul said.

"Okay, we all are. They're not after you. You just happened to be there."

Susan said, "One of the things I'm scared for is you." She was cutting celery up into a stainless-steel bowl that already contained white meat tuna fish. I reached across from the kitchen table and patted her hip.

"I got what I needed on Patty Giacomin this past weekend in New York."

Paul said, "What was it?"

I said, "This is tough. She went to New York each month to pick up strange men in the bar at the hotel."

Paul said, "Oh."

"I thought about not telling you that," I said. "But whatever we are doing, it doesn't work well on lying."

Paul nodded. Susan frowned. "There's nothing illegal in that."

"No, but Patty will bend to it. She won't want to look at herself in that light. It wouldn't help in custody or alimony fights, in the future. If any. It's enough ammunition for me."

Susan said, "Poor woman."

"Yeah, it's kind of tough to think about how desperate she was for whatever it was she thought she'd find. I don't assume she found it, that way."

"Promiscuity doesn't have to be a sign of unhappiness in a woman," Susan said.

"Once a month, in a distant city, with strangers, while drunk?"

Susan looked at Paul. "So why don't we call the police about these men shooting at us?" she said.

"It would be hard to explain without bringing in Mel and Harry and such. I don't want Mel in jail. I want him out earning money so he can support his kid and pay for his education and stuff."

"Yes, I see that." Susan mixed some mayonnaise into her tuna salad.

"I'll stay with you tonight, and tomorrow I'll see what I can do to wrap this thing up."

"What are you going to do about the contract?" Paul said.

"I'll probably have to talk with Harry about that," I said.

Susan nodded. "I knew that would come."

"You have a better thought?"

"No, it's just you're so predictable. You're going to talk with him because he shot at us. If it had just been you . . ." She shrugged.

"Well, I need to get him out of my way if we're going to get Paul into dance school."

Susan was putting tuna salad on whole-wheat bread. The coffee had stopped perking. Her shoulders were stiff and angry.

"I cannot let some gorilla shoot at you," I said. "I cannot. It's against the rules."

Paul said, "What rules?"

Susan said, "His. Don't ask him to explain them now. I can't stand it." She put the platter of sandwiches on the table and poured some coffee. "At least take Hawk with you," she said. "Will you do that? At least take Hawk. You have Paul to think of too." She took a carton of milk out of the refrigerator and poured Paul a glass. "And me," she said. Her hand shook slightly as she poured the milk.

" 'I could not love thee, dear, so much,' " I said, " 'loved I not honor more.' "

"Shit," Susan said.

CHAPTER 31

Susan took Paul with her to work. "He can read in my office waiting room," she said. "Until this is cleared up he won't be safe alone and probably not with you."

"It'll be cleared up quick," I said. "Next week, kid, we'll be back working on the cabin."

He nodded. Susan and Paul drove to the junior high school in her Bronco, the left side pocked with bullet holes. I followed in my MG. When I saw them safely inside, I drove back into Boston to my office. I needed time for sitting and thinking. I parked in my alley and went up the back stairs. When I got there, the door was ajar. I took out my gun and kicked it open.

A voice said, "Don't shoot, babe, it's Hawk." He was sitting in my clients' chair, tipped back against the wall out of the line of fire from the door. Hawk was never careless. I put the gun away.

"Didn't know you had a key," I said.

Hawk said, "Haw."

I went around my desk and sat down. "Cotton raise the ante?"

"Naw, I just come by to hang out with you, you know. I got nothing to do and I get restless. You wasn't at your apartment so I figured you'd come here."

I said, "Somebody tried to hit me at Susan's last night."

"She okay?" he said.

"Yeah, but that's not the gunny's fault."

"We gonna go see Cotton today," Hawk said. His face was impassive but the lines around his mouth seemed a little deeper and his cheekbones seemed a little more prominent.

I looked at him for a minute. "Yeah," I said. "We are."

Hawk stood up. "May as well get an early start," he said. I nodded. I took out my gun, spun the cylinder so there was a slug under the hammer, put a fresh slug in the chamber I usually kept empty under the hammer, and put the gun back on my hip. We went out. I locked the office door, and we went down the back stairs.

In the alley I said, "Where you parked?"

"Down front of your place," Hawk said.

"I'm right here," I said. "We'll take mine."

We got into the MG. Hawk pushed the passenger seat back further. "Cute," he said. We drove down Berkeley and turned west onto Commonwealth. The trees were leafing and brownstone town houses were bright with early flowering.

As we went through Kenmore Square, Hawk said, "You gonna have to kill him."

"Harry?"

"Uh-huh. You can't scare him."

I nodded.

"He near put a hole in Susan," Hawk said.

I nodded. About a block short of Harry's used-car

lot I pulled in and parked in a loading zone. We got out.

Hawk said, "I think I might drift around back, case they see you coming."

I said, "You know the place?"

"I been in there," Hawk said.

I nodded. Hawk turned down a side street, and cut through an alley and disappeared. I walked straight up Commonwealth and into Harry's office. Harry was at his desk. Shelley and two others were in the service bay. When I came in the door, Harry reached into the desk drawer for a gun. He got it out and half raised when I reached across the desk and slapped it out of his hand. Then I took him by the shirt front with both hands and yanked him out of his chair and frontward across the desk. Shelley yelled, "Hey," from somewhere to my left and then I got a dark glimpse of Hawk between me and the sound of Shelley's voice. I dragged Harry across the desk and slammed him against the far wall of the cinder-block office. He grunted. I pulled him away from the wall and slammed him back against it. He was kicking and clawing at me but I didn't notice much. I shifted my right hand from his shirt to his throat and jammed him against the wall, holding him up by the throat with his feet off the floor.

"Which one shot at us last night?" I said.

Harry swatted at my face. I ignored it and leaned my hand in against his windpipe. "Which one?"

He pointed at Shelley. I dropped Harry and he slid down the wall and sat gasping on the floor. I turned toward Shelley. "If you can get past me," I said, "Hawk won't shoot. You're out of here free."

Shelley and two others stood motionless against the wall in the repair section. Hawk with his gun steady and relaxed stood in front of them. There were three pistols on the floor. Shelley looked at Hawk. Hawk shrugged. "Okay by me, Shell. You ain't gonna make it by him anyway."

"Yeah, if I win you shoot me."

"You don't try and I shoot you now," Hawk said.

One of the other two men was Buddy Hartman. I said to him, "Buddy, take your pal and beat it. You ever come near me or anyone I know, I'll kill you."

Buddy nodded. His companion was a lean, dark, handsome man with the dark-blue shadow of a recently shaven heavy beard. His companion nodded too and they went past me and out the door of the gas station and down the street, walking fast without looking back. Hawk shook his head. "Should have burned them," he said.

Shelley stared after the two men who had gotten out. Then he lunged toward me, trying for the door. He weighed more than I did and the force of his lunge pushed me back against the doorjamb. I got a short uppercut in under his jaw and straightened him up with it slightly. Hawk leaned against the far wall with his arms crossed, the revolver still in his right hand. To my left, Harry Cotton was inching along toward his desk. I hit Shelley again under the jaw, and he stepped back and swung at me. I shrugged my shoulder up and took the punch on it. I hit Shelley four times, three lefts and a right in the face. He stumbled back, blood rushing from his nose. I hit him another flurry. He stumbled, waved an arm at me, and backed into Harry's desk. His hands dropped. I hit him one big left hook and a haymaker right hand and he went backward over the desk and hit the swivel chair. It broke under his weight and he lay still on the floor with one foot still on the desk. Harry was trying to get the gun I'd knocked away from him. It was partly under Shelley's body. I took a step around the desk and kicked Harry in the neck. He fell backward and made a swacking noise. I stood over him.

I said, "Never come near anybody I know. Never send anybody else. You understand me?"

Hawk said, "Ain't good enough. You gotta kill him."

"That right, Harry? Do I? Do I have to kill you?"

Harry shook his head. He made a croaking sound.

"You gotta kill him," Hawk said.

I stepped away from Harry. "Remember what I told you," I said.

Hawk said, "Spenser, you a goddamned fool."

"I can't kill a man lying there on the floor," I said.

Hawk shook his head, spit through the open door into the repair bay, and shot Harry in the middle of the forehead.

"I can," he said.

CHAPTER 32

Mel Giacomin's office was on a side street just off Reading Square. It was a private home that had been remodeled as an office. The secretarial pool sat out front in a big open room, and Mel and a couple of other men had private offices down the hall. Past Mel's office was the kitchen, which had been left intact, and there were cups and a box of doughnuts and instant coffee and Cremora on the kitchen table. Mel was in there drinking coffee when I showed up.

"What the hell do you want?" he said.

"Clever repartee," I said.

"What?"

"I want to talk about fire insurance," I said.

"I don't want to sell you any."

"It's about fire insurance you've already sold, like to Elaine Brooks."

Mel looked at me. He opened his mouth and closed it. "I didn't . . ." he started. "I . . ." A woman with red hair in a frizz came into the kitchen. She wore a lime-green sweater and a pair of white pants that had been tight when she was ten pounds lighter.

"Let's talk in your office," I said.

Giacomin nodded and I followed him next door. We went in. He shut the door.

"What do you want?" he said when he got behind

his desk. He was wearing a tan glen plaid three-piece suit and a blue-figured tie and a white shirt with light tan-and-blue double stripes in it. The vest gapped two inches at the waist, revealing belt buckle and shirt.

"I'll make it short," I said. "I know the arson scam. And I can prove it."

"What are you talking about?"

I took out the copy of my arson file memo and put it on his desk.

"Read this," I said.

He read it over quickly. I noticed that his lips moved very slightly as he read. Then his lips stopped. He was through reading it, but he kept staring down at the paper. Finally, without looking up, he said, "So?"

"So I got you," I said.

He kept staring at the paper. "You tell the cops?"

"Not yet."

"You tell anybody?"

"Don't even think about that," I said. "You don't have a chance against me, and even if you did, note that you're looking at a copy."

"You want a piece of the action?"

I grinned, "Now you are catching on."

"How much?"

"It'll vary."

He looked up. "What do you mean?"

"It means I want two things. I want you to stay away from your kid, and I want you to pay for his support, his schooling, whatever he needs."

"Stay away?"

"Relinquish, leave alone, get off the back of, fill in your own phrase. I want him free of you."

"And send him money?"

"Yes."

"That's all?"

"Yes."

"Nothing for you?"

"No."

"How much I gotta send him?"

"Tuition, room, board, expenses."

"How much will that be?"

"We'll let you know."

"I mean I'm not made of money, you know?"

I stood up and leaned over the desk. "Listen to me, Rat Shit, you're talking like you could bargain. You can't. You do what I say or you take a big fall. Two people died in one of those fires. Homicide in the commission of a felony is murder one."

"I didn't . . ."

I hit the desk with the palm of my hand and leaned a little closer so my face was about three inches from his. *"Don't bullshit,* you keep saying *didn't* to me and you'll be down to Walpole doing the jailhouse rock for the rest of your goddamned life. Don't *didn't* me, creep." *Not bad, me and Kirk Douglas.* I wondered if the palm slamming was overacting.

It wasn't. He folded like a camp chair. "Okay, okay. Sure. I'll go for it. It's a good deal."

"You bet your ass it's a good deal," I said. "And if you don't stick to your end of it, you'll boogie on down to Walpole faster than you can say first degree murder. And, I may stick my thumb in your eye before you leave."

"Okay," he said. "Okay. How much you want to start?"

"I'll bill you," I said. "And if you think when I

leave you can call Harry Cotton and have me taken away, you are going to be disappointed."

"I wasn't thinking that," Giacomin said.

"Bills are due upon receipt," I said.

"Yeah, sure. On receipt."

I straightened up and turned and walked out the door. I closed it behind me. I waited about thirty seconds then I opened it again. Giacomin was on the phone. When I looked in he hung up suddenly.

I nodded. "Rat shit like you is predictable," I said. I leveled a forefinger at him. "Don't mess with this, Melvin. Maybe it won't be Walpole. Capital punishment is regaining favor."

He sat and looked at me and said nothing. I left the door open this time and walked away without looking back.

I drove into Boston. Disco Stephen lived in Charles River Park and I still had Patty Giacomin to talk with. I parked on Blossom Street and walked down.

Patty Giacomin let me in. Stephen was there too in a faded Levi's shirt and jeans, and artfully broken-in over-the-ankle moccasins with big leather stitching. There was a leather thong tight around his neck. He was sipping from an enormous brandy snifter.

"What do you want?" she said. She was carrying a snifter twin to Stephen's.

"Christ, it must run in the family," I said.

"What?"

"Clever repartee."

"Well, what *do* you want?"

"We need to talk alone."

"I have no secrets from Stephen."

"I bet you do," I said. "I bet you don't share too many of your adventures in the New York Hilton with Old Disco."

Her head lifted a little. "I beg your pardon?" she said.

"Can we speak privately for about five minutes?"

She paused for a long time then she said, "Certainly, if you insist. Stephen? Could you?"

"Certainly," he said. "I'll be in the bedroom if you need me."

I let that pass.

When he was gone, she walked over to the window and looked down at the river. I walked with her. When we were as far as we could get from where Stephen could hear, she said softly, "You rotten bastard, what are you doing to me?"

"I'm telling you I know about how you used to go down to the New York Hilton once a month and screw whatever came by."

"You rotten prick," she said softly.

"Oh," I said. "You've found out."

She didn't speak. Her face was very red. She drank some brandy.

I said, "I've made a deal with your husband on whom I also have the goods. He stays away from Paul and pays his bills, and I keep my mouth shut. I'm offering you an even better deal. You stay away from him and I keep my mouth shut. You don't even have to pay any money."

"What goods have you got on him?"

"Zero in on the important stuff, babe."

"Well, what?"

"That's not your problem. Your problem is whether you do what I ask or I start blabbing to the like of Disco Darling down the hall."

"Don't call him that. His name is Stephen," she said.

"Will you stay away from the kid?"

"My own son?"

"That's him, you've got the right one. Will you?"

"What do you mean, stay away?"

"I mean let him go away to school, let him spend holidays with me, or where he wants to, make no attempt to claim custody or make him live with you or your husband."

"My God, just so you won't tell about one indiscretion?"

"Monthly indiscretions—random, promiscuous. Actually, probably neurotic. If I were you, I'd get some help. Also, if you don't do what I say, you get not another penny from your husband, alimony, nothing."

"How can you . . ."

"Call him," I said. "See what he says."

She looked at the phone.

"So there you'll be," I said. "Alone and broke. Disco Steve will roll you like a buck's worth of nickels if he thinks you're messy."

"It's not neurotic," she said. "If a man did it, you'd say it was normal."

"I wouldn't, but that doesn't matter to me. I want that kid out of the middle and I'll do what needs to be done to get him out. You go along or you're broke and abandoned like they say in the soap operas."

She looked down the hall where Stephen had disappeared. She looked at the phone. She looked down at the river. And she nodded her head.

"Do I hear a yes?" I said.

She nodded again.

"I want to hear it," I said.

"Yes," she said, staring at the river.

"Okay," I said. "You and Stephen can go back to watching his jeans fade."

I started for the door. "Spenser?"

"Yeah?"

"What did Mel do?"

I shook my head and went out and closed the door.

CHAPTER 33

Paul sat astride the ridge pole of the cabin, nailing
the final row of cedar shingles four inches to the
weather. He was shirtless and tan and the muscles
moved on his torso as he took the wide roofing nails
one at a time from his mouth and drove them three
to a shingle with the hammer. He wore a nailing
apron over his jeans and periodically he took some
nails from it and put them in his mouth. I put together the ridge cap on the ground. When he was finished with the final row, I climbed the ladder with
the ridge cap and we nailed it in place, working from
each end and moving toward the center of the ridge.
The early fall sun was warm on our backs. At the
center I said, "You drive one on that side and I'll
drive one on this."

He nodded, took an eightpenny nail out, tapped it
into place, and drove it with three hammer swings. I
drove mine. We slipped the hammers into his hammer holster and I put out my hand, palm up. He
slapped it once, his face serious. I grinned. He
grinned back.

"Done," I said.

"On the outside," he said.

"Okay, half done," I said. "Enclosed."

We scrambled down the ladder, me first, Paul after,

and sat on the steps of the old cabin. It was late afternoon. The sun slanting along the surface of the lake deflected and shimmered in formless patches when we looked at it.

"I never thought we'd build it," Paul said.

"Never thought you'd run five miles either, did you?"

"No."

"Or bench press a hundred fifty pounds?"

"No."

"Or put on twenty pounds?"

Paul grinned at me. "Okay," he said. "Okay, you were right. I was wrong. You want to have an award ceremony?"

I shook my head. There was very little breeze and the sweat on our bodies dried slowly. On the lake someone water-skied behind a hundred hp outboard. There were bird sounds in the close woods. The area was strong with the smell of sawn wood and the faint burnt odor that a power saw produces when the blade dulls.

I got up and went in the cabin and got a bottle of Moët & Chandon champagne from the refrigerator and two clear plastic cups from the cupboard. I put some ice and water into a cooking pot and stuck the champagne in to keep cold. I brought it and the plastic cups out onto the back steps and set it down.

"What's that?" Paul said.

"Champagne," I said. "Elegantly presented."

"I never had champagne," Paul said, "except that time at Susan's."

"It's time again," I said. I opened the bottle and poured each cup full.

"I thought the cork was supposed to shoot up in the air."

"No need to," I said.

Paul sipped the champagne. He looked at the glass. "I thought it would be sweeter," he said.

"Yeah, I did too when I first tried it. It grows on you though."

We were quiet, sipping the champagne. When Paul's glass was empty he refilled it. The water skier called it quits and the lake was quiet. Some sparrows moved in the sawdust around the new cabin, heads bobbing and cocking, looking for food, now and then finding it. Grackles with bluish iridescent backs joined them, much bigger, swaggering more than the sparrows, with a funny waddling walk, but peaceable.

"When do we have to leave tomorrow?" Paul said.

"Early," I said. "Eight thirty at the latest. We pick up Susan at eleven."

"How long a ride to the school?"

"Four hours."

"How come Susan's going?"

"After we drop you, we're going to have a couple of days together in the Hudson Valley."

What breeze there was had gone. It was still, the sun was almost set. It wasn't dark yet, but it was softer, the light seemed indirect.

"Do I have to have a roommate?"

"First year," I said.

"When can I come home? Back home? To see you?"

"Any weekend," I said. "But I'd stay around out there for a while. You need to get used to it before you come back. You won't settle in if your only goal is to get out."

Paul nodded. It got darker. The champagne was gone.

"It's better than that place in Grafton."

"Yes."

"Everybody there will know everyone and know how to dance."

"Not everybody," I said. "Some. Some will be ahead of you. You'll have to catch up. But you can. Look what you did in one summer."

"Except I wasn't catching up on anything," Paul said.

"Yeah, you were."

"What?"

"Life."

The woods had coalesced in the darkness now. You couldn't see into them. And the insects picked up the noise level. All around us was a thick chittering cloak of forest. We were alone at its center. The cabin was built and the champagne bottle was empty. Biting insects began to gather and swarm. The darkness was cold.

"Let's go in and eat," I said.

"Okay," he said. His voice was a little shaky. When I opened the door to the cabin I could see in the light from the kitchen that there were tears on his face. He made no attempt to hide them. I put my arm around his shoulder.

"Winter's coming," I said.

HERE'S A PREVIEW OF SPENSER'S TRIP TO LAID-
BACK, LARCENOUS L.A.—YOU CAN GET THE WHOLE
STORY NEXT MONTH IN *A SAVAGE PLACE*.

He looked at Candy and said, "Come on, you and
your date take a ride with us."

Candy looked at me. I said "Nope."

Franco looked at me for the first time. "I wasn't
asking ," he said. "Get moving, huh?"

I said "Nope" again. It had a nice rhythm to it.

Bubba had moved a little to Franco's right, but
neither showed a weapon yet. That's one of the
mistakes tough guys make. They overrate how tough
they are. They aren't careful.

I took the gun out from the cushions and pointed
it at them. No harm in being careful. I said "Nope."

Franco and Bubba looked at the gun. So did
Felton. His face got sweaty. Candy didn't move. She
seemed inside a kind of deep stillness.

"We have here," I said to Candy, "persuasive
evidence of complicity between Felton and Franco,
and of course the legendary Bubba. Bubba is on
hourly wage, I suspect, and doesn't count for much.
But I think we could make something pretty good out
of these other two."

"What can we really prove?" Candy said.

"We can prove Franco beat you up. We can prove
when we came here to talk with Sam Felton about
Mickey, he called Franco, and Franco came and
attempted to remove us. The threat of force was
clearly implied."

"I want it all," Candy said.

"Cops can get it all if we give them this," I said.
"Felton here will melt like butter on a flapjack when
Samuelson gets him down to the Hall of Justice. So

would Bubba, but he probably doesn't know anything."

"Don't get to feeling too good about that gun, huh?" Franco said. "I seen guns before. It ain't going to buy you all that much."

"If you do anything incautious," I said, "it cay buy you the farm."

Candy seemed not even to hear Franco. She barely heard me. She was way inside somewhere. "I want it all," she said again. "I want to get it myself." She was looking right at Franco now. "Did you shoot Mickey?" she said.

Franco made small grin. "Sure," he said.

"You shot him?"

"Yes, I just said so, huh?"

Bubba edged slightly more to the right.

I said, "Don't do that, Bubba. I'm good with this. I'll drop you where you stand."

Franco said, "And while you're shooting him, what do you think I'll be doing, huh?"

I said, "I can drop him and you before you can clear the piece. You made one mistake coming in here with your hands empty. Don't make another one."

Candy said, "You can't shoot him, Spenser. He's our key to the whole story."

I said, "Yes, I can. We've still got Felton," and then everything went to hell. The Mexican woman walked in through the archway and stopped next to Franco when she saw the gun. Franco stepped behind her. I raised my gun. Candy said "No" and pushed at my arm. Franco was around the corner of the archway. Bubba had his gun out. I yanked my arm free of Candy and shot Bubba twice and shoved Candy down on the sofa and sprawled over her, facing the archway. The Mexican woman was crouched on the floor near the archway. Felton was still cross-legged on the opposite couch, body bent as close to double as he could get, both hands over his head. Bubba had fallen backward to the floor. The smell of gunshot was in the room but no sound. The hum of central air conditioning filled an otherwise soundless void. Candy was motionless beneath me.

Then Franco's voice came from behind the archway. "Come on, Felton," Franco said. "Get off the couch and walk over here."

Felton kept his hands clutched over his head and looked up in my direction.

"Come on," Franco said again. "He won't shoot. He needs you alive, don't you, boyfriend. You kill him and you got nothing. Besides, I can blast the Mex from here and not even move. So we'll trade. Felton walks and you get the Mex, huh?"

Felton's voice was squeaky. "I'm coming." He got off the couch and scurried over to the archway and through.

I didn't speak. I could hear Candy's breath coming a little short beneath me. I could smell her perfume too, now that the shooting fumes were beginning to thin. I heard shuffling sounds recede down the front hall, then the front door opened and closed. I didn't move. Franco could open the front door and shut it without leaving, and when I came charging through the archway, he could cut me in half.

Then I heard the front door open again and shut. And silence. A double fake? Faintly I heard a car door slam. No double fake. I rolled around the corner of the archway in a crouch. Franco could have sent Felton out to start the car. The hall was empty. I opened the front door and watched the taillights of a car disappear up the street. I went back into the living room and looked down at Bubba. There was blood on his chest and his eyes were wide and silent.